REMEMBER ME WHEN

THE UNFORGETTABLE DUET, BOOK TWO

BROOKE BLAINE

Copyright © 2018 by Brooke Blaine

www.BrookeBlaine.com

All rights reserved.

No part of this book may be reproduced in any form or by any electronic or mechanical means, including information storage and retrieval systems, without written permission from the author, except for the use of brief quotations in a book review.

This book is a work of fiction. Names, characters, places, and incidents either are products of the author's imagination or are used fictitiously. Any resemblance to actual persons, living or dead, events, or locales is entirely coincidental.

Remember Me When

Cover Designer: ShanoffiDesigns

Cover Photographer: Darren Birks Photography (CoversUnleashed.com)

Cover Model: Zak Leete

SYNOPSIS

THE UNFORGETTABLE DUET

Three sugars, two creamers.
That's how you took your coffee every morning at Joe's Grab 'N Go.
But you don't remember that.
You don't remember anything.
Anything, that is, except me...
That day...
And the tragedy that catapulted us together.

Experience Ollie & Reid's journey in...

The Unforgettable Duet

Forget Me Not (Book One)

Remember Me When (Book Two)

True love always finds a way...

AUTHOR'S NOTE

Remember Me When is book two in The Unforgettable Duet.
If you have not yet read **Forget Me Not**, please close this book and begin book one, available at www.BrookeBlaine.com or Amazon.com.

CHAPTER ONE

REID

THREE MONTHS, TWO *weeks, and about*—I fiddled with the band of my watch as I glanced at the time—*two hours*. I hadn't intended to keep track of how long it'd been since I'd woken up from surgery, but I couldn't seem to stop from counting the days since my whole life had changed.

Or since I'd become *aware* that my life had changed, rather.

"Reid? Did you hear what I said?"

I blinked up at my mom, whose eyes were narrowed as she did a quick inspection to ensure I wasn't falling apart.

At least she wouldn't be able to tell anything was wrong from the outside.

I tried for a smile to appease her. "I'm sorry, what was that?"

"I said are you sure I can't take you tomorrow? To the Music Junction?"

Shaking my head, I sipped my coffee. "No, it's not that far from my apartment. I'll walk."

"But it's a couple of miles. And it'll be so muggy."

"It's fine."

A sigh escaped her as she tapped her fingers against her mug, and I could tell she was trying to hold her tongue. I hoped she would. My nerves were already shot from the couple of hours I'd spent under her intense scrutiny during Sunday breakfast, and it wouldn't take much more to send me over the edge. The problem was that I knew my mom too well. She was itching to say something else, to convince me I was being stubborn, and I should do what she thought was best.

Sure enough, a minute later, Mom gave in. "I just don't see why you won't let your father or me drop you by on our way to work. It'd be no trouble at all."

"Because it's unnecessary, and I have two legs that seem to be in working order."

Her frown deepened. "Reid... I know you're not ready to drive again, so I wish you'd let us help you. Honestly, I'd feel better if you'd let me—"

"Mom," I said, slapping the table with my hand, and my voice came out sharper than I'd intended, causing her to startle. Rubbing my forehead, I reined in my irritation, and when I spoke again, I made sure my tone was softer. "I've got it."

"Of course. Of course you do." She bit down on her lip, and her hands shook as she lifted the chipped ceramic mug my younger sister, Anna, and I had given her well over a decade ago that said "World's Best Mom." And she was. Really, she was. She'd been a saint through the endless weeks of recovery, as well as getting me set back up in my apartment, finding me a temporary summer job...

Sighing, I reached across the table for her, and when she lowered her mug, she placed her hand in mine. "I'm sorry. I don't mean to snap at you. I'm just ready for things to get back to normal."

"I know you are." She gave me a squeeze and wiped the corner of her eye. "I just worry about my baby boy, is all, and that won't ever change. When you're a parent, you'll understand."

"You don't have to worry about me. I'm fine."

A smile tipped her lips, seemingly appeased for the moment, until she looked down at the platter of food between us. "Oh dear. Either I made too many pancakes or you didn't eat enough."

"I had plenty. I'm sure dad or Anna will finish them off when they get home."

"You're right," she said, standing up and clearing our empty plates off the table. "Will you be joining us for church service this morning?"

I wiped my mouth as I got to my feet to help her. "No." The answer was always no. "Thank you for breakfast."

Mom's hopeful smile fell, and she set down the empty dishes before coming around the table to me.

"I love you," she said, reaching out to hold on to my arms. "And I'm sorry if I seem overbearing sometimes. You promise you'll tell me if you start feeling off or have any pain anywhere?"

I gave her a small smile. "Of course," I lied. I had to. I'd caused her more than enough worry to last a lifetime, and I could see the evidence in the dark circles under her eyes that she tried to cover with makeup, and the deep lines between her brows that seemed permanent when I was around.

She lifted her hand to the side of my face and stroked her thumb over my cheek. "You're my heart, Reid. I don't know what I would've done if we'd lost you."

The pain in her voice made me feel more than a twinge of guilt for losing my temper. I'd done that a lot lately. The psychologist I met with every week said it was completely normal to have feelings of distress after such a traumatic accident, but it didn't excuse biting off the heads of the people who cared about me. It wasn't like any of this was mom's fault.

None of it's your fault either, that quiet voice in the back of my mind tried to convince me, but I locked that thought away as Mom stood on her tiptoes to kiss my cheek.

"I'll take you back home on the way to service."

"Thank you," I said, not putting up a fight, since it would be a much longer walk to my place from theirs, not to mention it was raining out.

As we finished clearing the table, the front door opened and Anna came bursting through, while my father shook off the umbrella on the porch. When Anna saw me, though, she skidded to a stop.

"Oh. Hey, Reid." Her obvious discomfort at finding me there was a stab to the gut, and though I hated it, I understood why she was tentative around me. Of everyone, Anna seemed to have been hit the hardest by what had happened. They said when I woke up from the accident, I'd had no idea who she was. That somehow my memory of her had reverted to when she was a kid and I hadn't recognized the teenager she was now. But of course I didn't remember that, just like I didn't remember the accident or anything in the months afterward. How was I supposed to apologize for something I wasn't there for? But Anna and I had been close, despite the decade between us, and I hated that I'd hurt her in any way, hated that she was hesitant around me now, like she was waiting for me to forget her again.

"Hey, Banana," I said, using her nickname to greet her warmly as if there was no tension in the air. "Where ya been?"

"Um. At Emma's."

"Yeah? Toilet paper any houses?"

"Reid, don't give your sister any ideas," Mom called out from the kitchen.

I let out an exaggerated sigh. "Fine." Then I lowered my voice. "Did you sneak over to any boys' houses and play find the cherry pop?"

"Answer that, and I'm grabbing my shotgun," Dad warned her as he strolled back into the room and took a big bite of his rolled-up pancake.

That almost got a smile from her. "No. We went to the fair."

"Oh yeah?" I grinned. "Did you ride the Zipper until you puked like the last time we went?"

Anna's mouth dropped open and her hands went to her hips, typical teenage attitude position making her forget her introversion around me lately. "There was no puking. I'm seventeen now. I think I know better than to shovel in cotton candy before the ride." Her lips twisted. "But we did ride it, like, eight times in a row."

"Ugh, I feel nauseated already," I said, rubbing my stomach, and finally her smile creeped up.

"Anna." My father nodded in the direction of her bedroom. "We're leaving in ten."

"Yeah, okay. I'm going," she said, trudging off to get changed for church, but then she stopped and barreled back in my direction, surprising the shit out of me by wrapping her arms tightly around my neck.

I closed my eyes and squeezed her back just as tight. *I love you, Banana,* I thought.

"Not joining us?" my father asked, as Anna disappeared into her room.

I shook my head. "I've got some things I need to get done around the house."

He raised an eyebrow, but didn't attempt to call me out on my bullshit. But let's face it: we both knew I didn't have anything worth doing at my place. It was merely a respite from the curious glances and questions, as well as from the guilt. I only came to Sunday morning breakfast to appease my mom, who would've honked outside my place until I came down if I'd tried to refuse.

Twenty minutes later, I was back in the apartment my parents had fully furnished before I'd even set a foot inside last summer. I didn't feel much different now, an entire year later, than I had back then.

I hadn't wanted to come back to Floyd Hills. Hadn't wanted to put my teaching degree to use. I'd only gotten the damn thing as a backup in the first place, never intending to actually use it. But there I'd been, late last June. Broke as a joke from trying to make ends meet by traveling from city to city playing jazz standards to a restaurant crowd who never knew the difference between Thelonius Monk and Bill Evans.

Growing up, I always thought traveling and playing the piano for a living would make me happy. It'd been my dream for so long, but the reality had been a surprising wake-up call. I'd hated the cheap hotels, the only ones I could afford. The endless inebriated shouts for me to play "Piano Man." I hated that even with Natasha, my then-girlfriend, by my side, I'd never felt lonelier in my life. The only thing I'd truly loved in all of it was the music. In the handful of hours I played every night, I could escape the sad reality I didn't want to believe was mine.

God knows I tried to make it work, though, because to come home to Floyd Hills was to admit failure, and I wasn't a failure. But one look at me during a trip up to Nashville to watch my show, and my parents saw right through my act. The promise of helping me get on my feet with a steady job, my own place, a car...it was too alluring to say no to.

Which led me to where I was now. Even worse off than I was before, because, oh hey, let's throw in a girlfriend who doesn't wanna stick around, a car accident, maybe a few broken bones, a brain injury...and then, when he's supposedly all healed, let's fuck him up real good and make him undergo surgery again. Oh, and if we can toy with his memory so that he doesn't know what's real and what's not, let's do that too.

I scrubbed a hand over my face as I kicked off my shoes and tossed my keys onto the counter. The bottle of Crown in the bottom cabinet called out to me, but the last thing I needed was to lean on whisky as a crutch. Instead, I walked over to the living room window and shut the curtains to block out the sun that was trying to peek through the rain clouds.

The exhaustion that overcame me as I sank down into the couch had me closing my eyes, even though it was still midmorning. But, just like every time the darkness settled in, my mind screamed to life. Even when my physical body was dead tired, my subconscious raced, on a desperate search for answers. I knew all the pieces of the puzzle, the ones the doctors and my family had filled in, but none of it felt real. The last thing I remembered before waking up in a hospital room had apparently been months prior—the day of my accident. I'd overslept that morning and hadn't even had time to shave, because it was that or skip coffee, and working with kids required the caffeine boost. But…that was the last thing I could recall—leaving my apartment that day. Not getting into the red Mazda3 my parents had bought for me, not grabbing my usual at Joe's—nothing. The only thing that even remotely made sense to me was that maybe the crash was too painful to remember, so my mind had blocked it out. But what I couldn't understand was why the weeks afterward were also missing.

And sure, the time spent recovering from my injuries wasn't something I wanted to relive, exactly, but…something didn't feel right. The vague answers from my parents didn't add up, and they never kept eye contact with me when I asked about the weeks after the accident. It was like something was missing, something vital that no one was telling me, and my mind couldn't seem to rest until it knew what it was. The missing piece of the puzzle.

I pulled my phone out of my pocket and put on a piece by Bach to help quiet my thoughts, and then fluffed a pillow and put it behind my head. My last day of freedom and I was spending it passed out on my couch.

Pathetic.

Tomorrow I'd be rejoining the work force, although it was a baby step, since school was out for the summer. Tutoring kids in piano would be easy enough, and it would get me out of the house. Off this damn couch. And maybe, just maybe, give me some sense of normalcy.

Whatever that was.

CHAPTER TWO

OLLIE

THREE MONTHS AND way too many fucking hours. That was how long it'd been since I'd forced myself to walk out of Reid's life.

Not because I wanted to, but because after the surgery to repair bleeding in his brain, he'd woken up with no recollection of who I was.

None.

Zip.

Zero.

And I would never, ever forget his vacant expression as he looked at me.

"Who are you?"

My smile fell as I dropped my hand from reaching out for him and somehow managed to whisper, "What?"

Reid shifted himself up on the hospital bed. "Do I know you?"

His words made the blood in my veins go cold. That voice, so *curious and innocent, held none of the familiar warmth I'd come to know in the last few weeks.*

No. No, this isn't happening. He was playing a trick on me, and any second now, he'd crack a smile and say, "Gotcha."

Any time now, Reid. Any time...

But he kept watching me, and I kept standing there staring down at the man I'd fallen for, the one looking at me with no recognition whatsoever on his face. Soon, Reid's gaze shifted from me to the door, like he was uncomfortable with a stranger in his room.

A stranger...oh God.

Panic seized my chest, and I tried to rationalize. It's temporary, I told myself. He just woke up. Of course things are fuzzy. But in the pit of my stomach, I knew. I knew.

I was going to be fucking sick.

I ran a hand through my hair and swallowed back the bile that tried to rise in my throat as I struggled to come up with some explanation as to why I was there. "I, uh"—*my words came out hoarse, and I cleared my throat*—"work here. And was just coming by to check on...things."

"Oh." *Reid looked over at the vase of white lilies and blue hydrangeas that I'd set on the table by the window.* "You brought me flowers?" *he asked.*

Fuuuck. The flowers. How was I supposed to explain that if he had no idea who the hell I was?

I rubbed my chest, fairly certain what I was feeling had to be indicative of a heart attack. With any luck, I'd pass out in a few seconds.

A few seconds passed. No such luck.

"Someone was delivering those and asked if I'd drop them by." *Stupid. I mentally kicked myself as soon as I said it, but no explanation other than the truth came into my brain.*

"They're nice. Thanks for bringing them."

I swallowed. "You're welcome."

An awkward silence descended as I did a quick sweep of him, unable to help myself from checking to make sure he was otherwise okay. When my eyes landed back on his mesmerizing brown ones, I gave him a forced smile. I needed to leave. That much was painfully obvious.

"Is there...anything I can get you? Before I go?" I said.

"No. Wait, actually—"

This was it. The "gotcha" moment.

Reid squinted and held his hand up to shield his eyes. "If you could close the blinds, that would be great. It's a little bright."

"The blinds. Right." It took me a few beats to realize that meant move. With a numb body, I somehow shut all the blinds and made sure to grab the note from the flowers before he had a chance to read it and say, "Ollie who?"

I looked back at him before I got to the door. He'd pulled his covers up and his eyes were closed, already drifting off into a peaceful sleep.

He doesn't remember... He doesn't remember *me*...

As terrified as I'd been before his surgery, I'd never entertained the possibility that my time with Reid was over. It didn't seem real.

Any second now, I'd wake up and realize it was all a nightmare.

Any second now...

I never woke up.

With every day that passed, every phone call I made to his mom to check on him only to hear that, no, he still hadn't regained memory of anything since his accident, the hope I'd carried dwindled. Every day I called, every day Reid grew physically stronger, but the answer was always the same.

"No. I'm sorry, Oliver. The doctor said it's possible he may never remember," his mom had finally said. Fuck, I'd never forget that day. It had been a full month since Reid's surgery, and it was that day, and her words, that made it apparent Reid wasn't ever going to remember me. Maybe I needed to *somehow* let go.

"For now, maybe it's best if he concentrates on his recovery, on things that are familiar," she'd said. And I'd read between the lines: *without you*. Not that she'd been malicious about it, because God knew I understood, but the pain was almost physically unbearable.

My number was erased from his phone. And I'd drifted back into the life of complacency I'd had before Reid. Actually, scratch that. I was no longer complacent, not after knowing what life could be like with him. No, there was another term for what I was.

Fucking. Miserable.

Mike sang along with the Black Eyed Peas, rapping something about humps and lovely lady lumps, on Big Bertha's radio as he drove us back from a hospital drop-off, oblivious to my thoughts...or perhaps overcompensating for them.

"If you've got lady lumps, there's a conversation here that's long overdue," I said.

"Deb was singin' this song in the shower this morning, and now it's on the damn radio. I swear it's following me around. I can't get it out of my head." He flipped the channel to something with more twang. "Ah. That's better."

"Better is debatable."

Mike glanced over at me. "You know what you need? Something that'll perk you right up."

"If this is about you trying to convince me to go to the National Porn Star Conference again, I'm out."

"I wish you'd just think about it. Even Deb wants to go." I shot him a glare, and he rolled his eyes. "Fine. No porn stars. But for real, we gotta bring you back to life, my man. You used to be all cheerful and shit."

"I'm still cheerful," I muttered.

"Oh yeah? Smile for me, then."

I plastered on the biggest, fakest smile I could manage, and Mike reared back in his seat, cringing.

"On second thought, that'll give me nightmares," he said, and then turned into Joe's Grab 'N Go.

Sitting up straighter, I braced my hand on the door. "What do you think you're doing?"

"Listen, Ollie. I've skipped out on comin' here for months now, but I'm hungry, and you could use a decent cup of brew to help snap you out of that funk."

"For fuck's sake, I don't want to be here. And I'm not in a funk."

"Hmm. Yeah, you might need something a little stronger than coffee." As he put Big Bertha into park, he began to grind his hips on the seat and sang, "Oll-ieee needs a big...dick...right in his—"

"Okay," I said loud enough to cover the rest of his words. "Hurry up, then."

"Oh no, I'm not going without you."

"Mike—"

"Stop," he said, his humor fading. "Just stop being so scared and paranoid for one damn minute. You can't avoid this place because you think you'll run into Reid. And even if you do run into him one of these days, you're gonna have to face him sooner or later, because this town's too damn small for it not to happen eventually. And I know it's gonna hurt like fuck, but you're not a pussy. Are you? You a pussy?"

I snorted. "No."

"Good. Now get out of the rig."

When I didn't make a move, Mike leaned across me and popped the door open. With a sigh, I unhooked my seatbelt and climbed out, slamming the door after me for good measure. When he rounded the front of the rig, he put his arm over my shoulder and gave me a shake. "Atta boy. Make sure to apologize to Joe for hurting his feelings by not visiting."

Mike pulled open the door, and as we entered the convenience store, he called out, "Joe, my man. How the hell are ya?"

"Well, I'll be." Joe's face lit up, and he slapped his hand on the counter when he saw us. "Where you boys been?"

"Starving." Mike winked at him as he filled up a basket full of baked goods from the counter and then leaned over to put his hand on Joe's shoulder. "Good to see you, Joe."

The old man frowned and wagged his finger at us. "You're never too busy for coffee and cakes, you hear me? You gotta eat, or all these fritters will go to waste and I'll have to throw them out."

"Don't ever do that. We won't be staying away again." Mike nudged me. "Right, Ollie?"

"Uh, yeah. Right," I said.

"You better not," Joe said, as Mike gave him a salute and went off to grab a drink. "All of a sudden, three of my regulars, poof, gone. I tried not to take it all personal, you know."

My brow furrowed. *Me, Mike, and...?* "Three?"

"Mhmm. You two and there was another guy, but I heard he had a bad accident a few months back."

"You mean Reid?" Just being reminded of him made my chest ache.

"Yeah, you remember him? Such a nice fellow. Shame what happened to him."

"You, uh, mean he hasn't come in lately either?"

"No, but I can understand why. Heard he lost his memory and everything. Can you imagine? He probably doesn't even remember he drinks coffee, and I had a new latte machine all set up and everything."

As Joe continued to ramble on, all I could hear was that Reid hadn't been there. I'd assumed life would be back to normal for him, including his latte habit. All those months of avoiding this place only to learn he had been doing the same. Although maybe he wasn't purposely staying away like I was. Maybe he still didn't realize he liked coffee. Or maybe he wasn't recovering as well as I'd hoped.

Shit.

"Hey, Joe, you have any more of those onion ring chip things? You know what I'm talkin' about?" Mike asked, his voice carrying across the store.

"I do in the back. One second," Joe said, and then held a finger up. "Sorry, Ollie, I'll be back. Don't you be a stranger, now."

"I won't," I said, and this time I meant it. What a silly fucking thing to do, stay away from Joe's or anywhere because there was a remote possibility I could run into Reid. Hell, I *wanted* to see him, but what I didn't want was to see the way he'd look at me, like I was nobody in his world.

A fresh pot of coffee sat on the stand like it was ready for me, and I poured a big cup as I thought about the last time I'd been here. It'd been around the same time I'd stopped calling to check on Reid, something that made me feel guilty, though it had been at the request of his family. I could feel the note he'd given me before he went back for surgery burning a hole in my pocket, its words taunting me even now. Never did I leave the house without the folded piece of paper, and I felt conflicted even carrying it around when I hadn't exactly kept my promise.

"Excuse me." As an arm reached across me to place a travel mug under the latte spout, my entire body went still. I didn't even breathe.

I didn't have to look over to know it was him. I'd recognize his voice anywhere, know the scent of his shampoo mixed in with the light spray of cologne even from across a crowded room. But Reid wasn't across a room. He was standing beside me, and I'd been too caught up in my thoughts to notice his approach.

Just being near him again sent a flutter of excited butterflies through my stomach, and I couldn't stop myself from looking over at him. He almost took my breath away, he was so fucking handsome. His dark, almost black hair was still cut short, and he was as put together as ever in a pair of khaki pants and a polo shirt. God, it'd been so long since I'd seen him, touched him, and my hands itched to reach for him, to pull him into my arms and hold him there. Being so close made me ache for him so badly it hurt.

As if he felt my gaze on him, Reid looked up, and I quickly turned away.

"Hey," he said, "I know you."

Wait, what? "You do?"

"Yeah..." As his eyes narrowed, I held my breath. "You brought flowers to my hospital room, right?"

Heat flooded my face as I lowered my head and focused on stirring my coffee. "Uh, yeah, I think I might've dropped them by...for someone."

Wow. All the time we've spent together and I'm the flower delivery boy. Fuck me.

"Hey, Ollie," Mike shouted, and I glanced up to see him round the corner with a bag of chips in his hand. "Look, I found—Oh shit." He stopped in his tracks, his eyes wide as dinner plates, as he looked between Reid and me, and then he cleared his throat and thumbed toward the door. "I'll be in the rig...whenever..." He shot me an apologetic look and then hightailed it away.

Thanks a lot, asshole.

Reid cocked his head to the side and pursed his lips as he looked at me curiously. "Your name's Ollie?" His gaze dropped to my name etched on my shirt. "Oliver?"

"Yes. Both, but my friends call me Ollie."

"Huh."

"What?"

He chewed on his lip for a moment, and then slowly shook his head. "Nothing."

As he reached across me again for his mug, I wondered what that look had meant. But I didn't have time to think about it for long, because Joe caught wind of his long-lost customer and came barreling down the aisle, as fast as his limping gait could take him.

"Reid," Joe said, holding on to Reid's shoulders as he smiled at him. "What a treat, all three of my boys in the same day. Ollie and I were just talking about you. It's good to see you upright."

"Thank you. Good to be upright," Reid said.

"We've been prayin' for you every day. You know who I am, right?"

"Yes, I know who you are, Joe."

Joe beamed. "I tell ya, nothin' makes me happier than you rememberin' little ole me."

Ouch. He didn't mean any harm by his words, I knew that, but the fact that Reid knew who Joe was—*Joe, of all people*—but had no idea who I was other than some random flower delivery guy? Jesus, that hurt more than I cared to admit. I needed to get out of there before any more of my heart or ego got crushed.

"You saw the new latte machine, right?" Joe said to him, as I capped my coffee.

"I did. It's awfully fancy."

"Nothing but top of the line for the Grab 'N Go, I tell ya." Joe wrapped an arm around Reid's shoulders and pointed at the machine with his cane. "Did you see all the features on this one? It's even got a frother..."

Joe's spiel gave me the out I needed to sneak down the aisle before Reid was able to ask any other questions about why I'd really been in his hospital room, or why my job description as a paramedic, as evidenced on my shirt, wasn't exactly a position that worked inside the hospital, like I'd said. After paying for my drink, I snuck one last look at Reid.

He was here. He was okay. And even if he didn't remember me, he was alive. That was enough, right?

As soon as I opened the passenger door to Big Bertha, Mike let out a stream of apologies.

"I'm so sorry, Ollie. I swear to God, I never would've brought you by if I'd thought for a second that Reid showing up was any kind of possibility."

"It's fine." It wouldn't change anything even having seen him. But at least I'd *gotten* to see him, which was something, I supposed.

"But he looks good, right? Did you talk? I thought I interrupted you talking."

I sighed and leaned back on the headrest, no longer in the mood for coffee. "Just drive."

CHAPTER THREE

OLLIE

IT'D BEEN A long time coming, but it was finally time to fix the damn stoop.

I'd been trying to keep my mind off my run-in with Reid earlier in the week, and that meant finally doing a bit of work around the house and landscaping in the evenings. I had a full day planned, having already painted the shutters a refreshed hunter green, and after I got the porch step back in non-crumbling order, the door was next.

The sun blazed overhead, the weekend already off to a sweltering start at ten in the morning, and I had to wipe the sweat off my brow with my forearm as I worked. With a trowel, I carefully filled in the cracks of the brick step with mortar—and tried not to think about the polite way Reid had asked my name and made small talk, like I was a stranger. It was the way he used to look at me, but back then it hadn't caused a roll of nausea the way it did now.

Stop thinking about him for one fucking second, I thought, as I smoothed out the filled cracks. I should've brought out a radio.

"Hello, Oliver."

I jerked around at the woman's voice behind me, and when I saw who it was, I couldn't mask my surprise. "Mrs. Valentine?" I looked over her shoulder, half expecting to see Reid getting out of that SUV that I hadn't heard pull up in my driveway. *That's what's you get for being so lost in your thoughts about her son.*

"It's just me," she said, and it sounded like an apology. "I was hoping I could speak with you."

"Oh. Yeah, sure. Let me just clean this up." I swept off the excess mortar from around the brick and then packed up my toolbox and moved it to the side, out of view.

"I don't mean to interrupt—" she started.

"No, you're fine. I was finishing up anyway," I said, wiping my hands on my jeans. Mrs. Valentine looked picture perfect in a cream-colored skirt and pink blouse, and of course the day I had company I'd be dressed in the paint-splattered jeans I wore when I worked around the house. At least I'd managed a shirt today.

I headed up the stairs, sidestepping the one I'd been working on, and she did the same. Stepping inside the cool, air-conditioned house, I gestured for her to come inside.

She held her purse in front of her and smiled politely as she entered. "I should've called before intruding on you like this."

"It's no problem," I said, shutting the door behind her and leading her down the hall. "Can I get you something to drink?"

"No, thank you. I won't take up too much of your time. I just wanted to—" She came to a stop as the hallway opened up into the living and kitchen area, and her eyes landed on the piano in the corner of the room. "Oh," she said with a smile. "No wonder you and Reid got along. I didn't realize you played."

I rocked back on my heels. "I don't."

She whirled around to face me, a question forming on her lips, but when I straightened my shoulders and met her gaze head-on, I could see the instant the light bulb went off. Her hand came up to finger the gold cross necklace she wore as she looked away. "May I sit down?"

"Please." I gestured for her to sit anywhere. "Are you sure you don't want anything to drink?"

"No, I'm fine. Thank you."

As she perched on the edge of the couch, I went into the kitchen to towel off and wash my hands. Then I poured a big glass of water and sat down in the recliner, giving her a wide berth.

What had she come here for? I didn't even realize she knew where I lived.

"I found your address in the phone book," she said, answering my silent question as she placed her purse beside her and smoothed her skirt down. "I had no idea we were neighbors. Have you been here long?"

"A few years."

She nodded and looked around. "It's lovely."

"Thanks. Workin' on a few repairs, but"—I spread my hands—"it's home."

She smoothed her skirt again, and it occurred to me then that she was nervous, and that, in turn, made me nervous. Was she here because something was wrong with Reid? I couldn't imagine why else she'd track me down, and as I sat there waiting, my knee began to bob up and down. But still, she remained silent.

"I'm guessing you didn't come over to talk about my house," I said, hoping to prompt a response.

"No, I didn't." She went to smooth her skirt again, caught herself, and then clasped her hands together instead. "I'm sorry. I'm not sure where to start."

"Has Reid suffered another setback?"

Her eyes shot up to mine. "No. Well...physically he's fine."

"Physically?"

"Yes," she said. Fingering her necklace, she closed her eyes, and when she opened them again, they glistened with tears. "Oliver, I came here today because I'm worried about my son."

That sent my adrenaline pumping. "Why? What's happened?"

"I don't know. He tells me he's fine, but I don't... I don't think he is. He's just so different. Angry."

"Angry? Reid?" I hadn't caught a glimpse of that when I'd seen him on Monday.

"Yes. And the doctors say it's normal. The moodiness, the change in behavior, but it's been months now. He snaps at me, at his father, at the doctors. I'm at a loss for what to do. How to help him."

I finished off my water and set the glass on the coffee table. "Pardon me saying this, but your son has been through hell the last few months. I'd be pretty upset too, especially if my memory had been toyed with the way his has. I'd venture to say he probably doesn't know what's real, what's not, or if his brain really is okay."

"I know that. It's just...he remembers everything from before the accident, so for all intents and purposes, everything should be back to normal for him. Easier to understand. He *should* be fine."

"But he's not."

"No, he's not. I thought maybe it would help to have friends around, but a few have been over, guys that he used to be close with when he lived here before, but he won't have anything to do with them. I thought maybe Natasha, but..." She shook her head. "It's like he's lost interest in the things and the people he used to love. And I don't..." She choked on a sob and reached inside her purse for a packet of tissues. "I'm sorry," she said, pulling one out to dab her eyes. "I just don't know how to help him."

My heart squeezed at her pain, as well as what Reid and the rest of his family had to be feeling. *God.* The thought of Reid suffering in any way was gut-wrenching. I sat forward with my elbows on my knees, wanting to say something, wishing I had words that could help make her feel better. Help him to heal. But I was on the outside looking in, and I feared nothing I said or did could make a difference.

I was no one in his world. And that truth was devastating.

"He's moved back into his apartment. I think he sits in there and...well, I don't know what he does, to be honest. I'm afraid it's nothing good." She wiped the corner of her eye again. "When he's been over, his sister just runs out of the room, which I know doesn't help things. My boy is so lost."

Huh. It was strange; I thought he'd be back to the Reid I'd known—easygoing, even with the trauma he'd been through. Inquisitive. Forward. Not at all the withdrawn version his mom described.

"If he's trying to find ways to cope, whether it's anger or isolation...he's scared," I said. "It's probably not the best time for him to be on his own, but if he's pushing others away..." I was at a loss, and more than anything, I wanted to drive over to his apartment and somehow fix him.

"He's been through so much, and I know he wants to put all this behind him. We all do. But I'm afraid I'm down to desperate measures—"

"And I'm your last resort?" I finished.

Her dark eyes, so much like Reid's, widened. "I didn't mean it like that—"

"I know you didn't," I said, waving her off. "But tell me what I can do to help Reid." *I'll do anything.*

"I think... I think he could use a friend."

"A friend," I repeated. I stared at her for a long moment, wondering if that was all she thought we'd been. Hell, if he needed a friend, he could've chosen any of the ones she'd brought over, but he hadn't, had he?

She shook her head. "I'm sorry. What I meant to say was...I think he needs *you*."

"Me?" I blinked, sure I'd heard her wrong.

"Yes. *You*."

As her words washed over me, I couldn't help but think that this was some kind of alternate universe. After telling me she thought he should recover without me, now Reid's mom was over here asking me for help? Saying she thought Reid needed *me*? Even so, the quickest flash of hope went through me at the possibility of spending time with him again. But then I remembered our recent run-in, and I shut that down before it spiraled out of control.

"Look, I don't see how I could help. He doesn't have a clue who I am," I said.

"No, but maybe you could get to know him again."

Isn't that what he asked me to do? Help him remember?

"Are you sure that's what you and Mr. Valentine want?"

"We want what's best for our son."

"And you somehow think that's me?" I sighed and dropped my head into my hands. "I thought he'd be better off without me," I said quietly.

"He's not. I don't believe for a moment that that's true. At first we thought it would be better that he only be around things familiar so he could heal without any confusion. But he's not. Not healing, that is," she said, her voice wavering, close to tears. "I've never seen Reid happier than he was in the weeks following his accident. And I would've thought he'd be scared or angry then. Certainly he would've had every right to be. The only thing I can think of for the change in him is you."

My eyes blurred as she scooted to the edge of the couch then and put her hand over mine.

"Please, Oliver. If Reid means anything to you at all, help me get my son back."

I blinked, and hot tears trailed down my face as I wondered if I could be the one to help him at all. Not only that, but would I allow myself a repeat of the inevitable heartbreak that would come from getting close to Reid again? That question was one I could answer without hesitation—yes. There wasn't anything I wouldn't do for his happiness, even if that price came at the sacrifice of my own. But I told myself it was no sacrifice at all to know the man I cared about more than any in this world would be okay.

Once again, I thought of the note Reid had written before his surgery, and the way he'd told me not to give up on him. Christ, I hadn't even tried, had I? I'd let his family do what they thought best and sacrificed my feelings, but what if that had been the wrong decision?

There was no question in my mind what I wanted to do, but putting myself in Reid's path outside of Joe's would be tricky. I couldn't do anything that would scare him off, not if I wanted to build his trust again.

"I'll do it," I said, wiping my face with my sleeve. "But I'll need some help to figure out how best to break the ice with him."

"Actually"—Mrs. Valentine's gaze drifted to the piano—"I think I have an idea..."

CHAPTER FOUR

REID

H E WAS HERE. The guy I'd run into at Joe's, the one who'd been in my hospital room.

He was here. At the Music Junction, where I was spending my Sunday afternoon picking up a class for beginner pianists, since the usual instructor had gone on maternity leave.

Ollie. I couldn't shake why his name stuck out to me when we hadn't officially met in all the times we'd seen each other getting our coffees. Maybe just that it was an unusual name, but it was one I kept thinking about since I'd run into him at Joe's.

As he lingered in the doorway, I realized just how big of a guy he really was. Taller than me by at least a couple of inches, and so muscular that he looked like he'd bust out of the pale green shirt he wore. It was a wonder I'd never noticed his size before. Especially with the shock of wavy auburn hair that was combed back on top and buzzed on the sides, and matching scruff covering his jaw, chin, and upper lip. *Jesus, he could be a pro wrestler.*

He leaned back outside the door like he was checking the room number, confusion written all over his face. It was a look I'd seen plenty of times from the parents of new students, so being the one in charge, I walked over to help him out.

"It's Ollie, right?"

Like I'd shocked him with a Taser, he jerked his head back inside. "Yeah?"

I held out my hand. "I don't think we've officially met. I'm Reid Valentine. I'm taking over for Mrs. Bishop while she's out."

"Reid...right," he said, shaking my hand. "It's nice to meet you. Officially."

His grip was strong, his skin searing hot to match the scorching July weather.

"Are you dropping off?" I asked, as he pulled his hand back.

"Pardon me?"

"Your child. For the class."

"Oh. No, I don't have kids." Then he looked around the room at the under-eighteen crowd that dominated the class, and his eyebrows shot up. "Uh, is this a kids' class?"

Wait, was he here to *attend*? Really... "Not technically, no."

"What does that mean?"

"Well, it's open to all ages, but it's primarily filled with kids or teens who've been sent by their parents. We don't get too many adults." *If ever.*

"Oh." He ran a hand through his damp hair and looked ready to bolt.

"Are you here for the class?"

"I was. I mean, I am."

"Is this like a bucket list thing for you?"

"Uh...yeah. Something like that."

"Come on in, and I'll get you set up." I walked over to the piano at the front of the room and grabbed one of the sheets from the top. When I handed it to him, he looked down at the paper in confusion. "That's the lesson for today."

"This is the beginner's stuff?"

"It is." My lips twisted as I fought back a grin, because bless his heart, he was out of place. But I'd welcome anyone who wanted to learn an instrument, even if they were mid-thirties-ish and looked like they could bench-press me if I looked at them wrong.

"So, should I, uh...take a seat?" he asked.

"Yep, anywhere you like. We'll start in a few minutes."

"Okay, thanks."

He chose one of the pianos near the front, since a handful of teens had taken up residence at the ones in the back, and as he set the sheet music in front of him and wiped his hands on his jeans, I almost laughed. I had a feeling the kids were going to kick his ass at playing "Twinkle, Twinkle, Little Star."

Once everyone was inside, I went to the front of the room and whistled to get everyone's attention.

"All right, welcome, folks, to Piano for Beginners. My name is Mr. Valentine, and I'll be filling in until Mrs. Bishop gets back."

A couple of girls in the back giggled, and I ignored them. It was my name or age that seemed to get to them every time.

"Today we're going to be focusing on the song listed on the sheet I gave you as you came in, but first, I'd like to go over proper hand posture."

As I launched into the lesson, I went around the room to make sure everyone was positioned correctly and had their starting points. When I got to Ollie, I took his wrist and moved his hand over three keys.

"That's middle C," I said. "It's your center. You get lost and you come back here."

He looked up at me with eyes so light green they were almost clear. Damn. Were they always like that?

Ollie nodded. "My center. Got it."

Something in his gaze sent my stomach dropping, and I let go of his wrist like he was on fire.

That unsettled feeling remained as I continued on to the next student. What the hell was that? The guy had seemed friendly enough, and I didn't get any red flags popping up. I tried to put my reaction behind me as I continued on with the lesson. "Twinkle, Twinkle, Little Star" was the song they'd be learning to play today, and it was one of the easier ones to begin with. Or so I'd thought.

I didn't go near him again, keeping my distance, because my instincts told me there was something more to that guy than what he let on. Nothing dangerous...I didn't think. But I couldn't put my finger on it. Every so often I'd swear I felt the heat of his gaze, only to turn around and see him studiously watching his fingers as he hit the wrong key. And each time I looked over to see Ollie helplessly trying and failing to follow along, I had to fight back a grin. The poor guy, he didn't have a musical bone in his body, and I doubted he'd ever sat behind a piano before in his life. But he was trying, and in this class, that was all that mattered. It was kind of entertaining to watch, though.

The hour passed quickly, most everyone nailing the piece, and I went around the room, gathering up their music sheets.

"All right, that's all for today. Make sure to practice over the week, because we'll pick back up with it next week before moving on."

The kids couldn't get out of there fast enough, ready to get on with their summer outside of the classroom, and I couldn't blame them. I'd only given up my weekend as a favor to Mrs. Bishop, whose mom had been my own instructor when I was younger.

As I ventured over to where Ollie sat, I said, "Nice effort today."

"'Nice effort'? Is that something you say to students who fail miserably?"

"It's not failing if you try."

He shook his head, chuckling as he handed me his music sheet. "I definitely tried."

"Then you didn't do as badly as you think."

"Yeah? You know, you're a really good teacher. I had no idea what the hell I was doing, but you made it easier to follow. Well, somewhat."

I had to laugh. "Somewhat" was right. "Does that mean you'll be back next week for round two?"

A grin slowly crossed his lips. "Yeah, I think so. Unless you're making us play Beethoven in front of the class or something."

"That's the third lesson."

"Well, shit, I'd better get to practicing."

"You'll be playing at Carnegie Hall and putting us all to shame before you know it."

Ollie laughed. "I'm not delusional. I'm every bit as aware as you are that I have no talent for music whatsoever, but you made it fun."

"Thanks, I appreciate that."

As the silence descended between us, I became acutely aware that we were the only ones left in the room, and for some reason, that sent a flurry of nerves through me. *What is going on?* The guy wasn't even remotely threatening, especially from where I towered over him while he sat on the bench.

He had honest eyes and a friendly smile, for fuck's sake. I wanted to kick myself. Now, not only did I suffer from memory loss, but I was also projecting on random people. *I really am losing it.*

"Well," I said, straightening the papers on top of the piano, "I better shut things down here."

"Yeah, I should get going too." As Ollie rose to his feet, I noticed the color of his eyes again, and the way they matched his shirt.

Backing away, I tapped the stack on my hand and gave him a

tight smile before going over to the filing cabinet to put the music sheets away.

"Um." Ollie cleared his throat, and I looked over to where he stood by the piano at the front of the room. "I hope you don't mind me saying this, but I noticed you weren't driving the other day. Did you need a ride or anything?"

Not only was the guy perceptive, but he wanted to drive me home? Maybe I wasn't wrong to be wary. *Nah, he's just being nice.*

"Oh. No, that's okay," I said. "I've been walking. You know, getting in some exercise when I can."

"In this heat? That's crazy."

"Every bead of sweat is another calorie lost," I joked.

"What if you pass out on the way? Heat stroke is a real thing. Take it from me."

"I've spent a half-hour in a sauna before. I think I'll be okay."

"Are you saying no because of stranger danger? I promise I'm not a serial killer or anything."

"Gee, thanks for the assurance," I said, shaking my head, but I was smiling. "I feel so much better."

Ollie's smile dimmed and he tapped his fingers over the top of the piano. "No, but seriously. It's no problem at all to drop you home, and I'd worry less if I blasted you with my air conditioning."

"As nice as that sounds, I'll have to pass. I appreciate the offer, but I like to walk." *You're gonna regret that in about thirty minutes.*

Ollie looked like he wanted to say something else, but he just gave me a nod and smiled. "Be safe. I'll see you again soon, Reid."

"Sure thing."

As he walked out, part of me wished I would've taken him up on his offer, if only because my feet were starting to ache in these shoes, and he was right—it'd be a furnace outside. But no matter. It wasn't like I was in a hurry to get home anyway.

I grabbed my satchel and made sure the room was in order before flipping off the lights and locking the classroom door. Taking my earbuds out of my pocket, I waved to the weekend receptionist and then pushed open the glass door that led outside.

As soon as I did, I was tempted to haul ass back inside. It wasn't a quick summer shower, it was a torrential downpour that had me seeking shelter under the awning. The water covering the parking lot was already deep enough to soak a man's socks, and as I looked down at my pressed slacks and shoes, I knew they wouldn't be surviving the long walk home.

Great. The one day I hadn't checked the weather, and it was a freakin' monsoon outside. *Not the way I want my day going.* I thought about calling my parents, but I struck that idea down. Let them pick me up this time and they'd do it every time, and that wasn't how I wanted to earn back my independence. I reached into my pocket for my cell phone to call an Uber, but cursed when I realized I'd left it on my kitchen counter.

A figure running across the parking lot caught my attention. Ollie hadn't brought an umbrella either, and his clothes were already soaked through as he got to his car. As he backed out and headed toward the exit, I dashed out under the awning and waved my arms to get his attention. It was against my better judgment, and I didn't really know the guy, but fuck it. I wasn't walking home in this storm.

Ollie slowed to a stop next to me under the covered area and lowered his window.

"So," I said, shaking the rain out of my hair, "how about that ride?"

CHAPTER FIVE

REID

AS SOON AS I shut the door, trapping myself in an enclosed space with Ollie, I began to think that this had been a bad idea. The strange feeling in my stomach was back, and it occurred to me then that I'd gotten in a car with a guy I really didn't *know* at all.

It's a two-mile drive. He's not gonna pack you in the trunk. Calm the hell down.

"Little wet out there," Ollie said with a laugh as I buckled in.

"Yeah, I wasn't expecting rain, or I would've come better prepared."

"Me too." He wiped his face with his hand and then ran it through his hair. The rest of him was soaked as well, making his clothes stick to his skin.

Jesus, he's ripped. With his shirt clinging to his massive chest and biceps, he somehow looked even bigger. Or maybe it was just the way he filled the small space we were in.

Why am I even noticing another guy's muscles? That's fucking weird.

Ollie put the car in drive. "Where to?"

"The Garden Lakes complex."

"Okay."

"You know where that is?"

"I do. Why do you seem surprised?"

I shrugged. "It's kinda hidden, I guess. My friends were always missing the turnoff."

"Ah." Then after a pause, he said, "I had a boyfriend who lived over there."

That made me do a double take. A boyfriend? He was gay? I don't know why that news left me dumbstruck, but it did. "Had? Did it end badly?"

As we pulled up to a red light, Ollie looked my way with sorrow in his eyes. "Yeah. You could say that."

"I'm sorry."

"It's not your fault," he said as the light turned green and his focus returned to the road.

"Breakups are the worst. I mean, how do you go from being so close to someone to practically a stranger overnight? You know?"

He white-knuckled the steering wheel and stared straight ahead. "Yeah. I'm still figuring that out."

Okay, I'd obviously steered us into an uncomfortable topic. It was one I wondered about often, though. I'd seen my ex, Natasha, recently, but it felt as though I was talking to someone I'd just met. It was hard to believe I'd spent years of my life with her when it all felt like a blur.

"Reid?" Ollie said. "Would you do me a favor?"

"Uh, sure."

"Close your eyes."

"Close my eyes? Why?"

"Just trust me."

Something in his voice made me want to obey, so I did as he said. I shut my eyes.

"Keep them closed until we're clear," he said.

"Until we're clear of what?"

"If I told you, it would negate the reason for you to have them shut in the first place."

"Ollie—"

"Please, Reid."

Please, Reid. There'd been an edge of alarm in his words, and that had me wondering what the hell was going on. But I kept my eyes closed and leaned back, listening to the rain as I waited for him to give me the okay.

A few seconds later, red and blue lights flickered against my lids, and they opened involuntarily before I had a chance to process what those colors actually meant.

The scene in front of us was like something out of a horror movie. There were police cars everywhere, fire trucks, at least two ambulances that I could see, but it was the wreckage in the middle, three cars piled up against each other, that had my heart stopping.

Then there was a flash in my memory, of something slamming into me, glass shattering, the air bags detonating from all around.

"Oh my God," I said, as my chest seized. Suddenly I couldn't get enough air. The sight of the mangled cars, the rescue lights flashing... It felt all too familiar. Too much to take.

Ollie's voice cut through the images that wouldn't stop playing. "Reid, I'm gonna need you to bend over and put your head between your knees. Do it now."

I tried to catch my breath, but the panic attack was strong. Ollie's hand went to my back as I leaned over and gasped for air.

"It's okay," he said, soothing me like one would a frightened animal. "They've got it under control. You're in here and you're safe."

But I didn't feel safe. My right side felt like someone had taken a bat to my ribs, and my head hurt something fierce.

This isn't real. Breathe. Just breathe.

I was vaguely aware of Ollie talking me through it, and a few seconds later, he'd shoved a bag under my nose for me to breathe into.

Steady breaths. *It's not real. I'm alive. There's no pain. It's not real.*

I had no idea how long I stayed bent over, struggling to right my world once again, but the whole time Ollie's hand stayed on me, his presence keeping me grounded.

As my breaths began to slow back to normal, I pulled the bag away and I dropped my head into my hands. "Fuck."

"It's okay. Let it pass. There's no rush."

I couldn't seem to think of anything other than the wreckage, the one we'd just seen as well as the one my mind was showing me. Had that been me in that car, lying on top of an air bag? It seemed real but...not. Like I was watching it happen but could still feel the pain. Was it real or was my brain making shit up now?

Was I going crazy?

After a while, I sat back up, and Ollie held out a travel cup. "Would you like some water?" he asked.

Nodding, I took the drink gratefully. There was still ice inside, and the cold water was a shock to my system—one that was much needed. It was then that I also realized that he'd kicked the air up and positioned the vents to blow directly on me. Not only that, but he'd pulled us into an empty parking lot far enough away that the accident was no longer visible.

"Fuck," I said, wiping my mouth. "I'm sorry."

"Don't be. Just drink some more."

I took another couple of deep gulps before handing the cup back to him. My heart wasn't jackhammering anymore, and with the air blowing on my face, I could breathe again.

Leaning back against the headrest, I said, "How did you know?"

"Know what?"

"You asked me to close my eyes. How did you know that accident would set me off?"

Ollie's eyes penetrated mine. "Do you want the truth?"

"Yes."

"Because I was there."

"You were where?"

He dropped his arm from the steering wheel to stroke the scruff on his jaw. "I'm a paramedic. I was there the day of your accident. As a matter of fact, I'm the one who got you out of the car."

His words sucked the air from out of the small space, and I felt my mouth fall open. "What did you just say?"

"You heard me."

"You—" The words got stuck in my throat. Ollie was the one who'd saved me? Ollie?

"I know that's probably surprising. It was a hell of a shock to get the call that morning and see that it was you."

"I-it was?"

"Yeah. I'd seen you about ten minutes before at Joe's while we were getting coffee. It wasn't exactly how either of us pictured our mornings going, I imagine."

"Wow." That was all I could manage as I let that information sink in. "I don't know what to say."

"You don't have to say anything. I just thought you should know."

In a daze. That was how my head felt. "Was it as…bad…as the one back there?"

"We got you out. That's all that matters."

"I heard the driver that hit me walked away fine."

"A bit of whiplash, but yeah."

"Huh." I crossed my arms and stewed about that fact for the millionth time.

"You can say it."

"What?"

"What you're thinking. That it doesn't seem fair that the accident was his fault and yet you're the one suffering."

"How'd you know that's what I was thinking?"

"Because I would be. Doesn't make you a bad person to have those thoughts."

It was like he could read my mind. Even though I tried not to think about it, knowing someone else's rush to get to work had upended my entire life for the worse... It was hard not to be bitter. But yeah, that's what I was. Bitter.

"You're right," I said. "I feel..."

"Yeah?"

"Pissed the fuck off."

Ollie's mouth quirked up on one side. "I'd be more worried if you weren't."

"Really?"

"Yeah."

"I'm guessing you see this kind of thing a lot."

"More than I'd like to."

"So how do you do it? You see all this bad shit every day and you don't seem jaded by it at all."

"Trust me, I have my days. More often than not lately," he said, his focus moving to the window. "But at the end of the day, I'd like to think I've helped in some small way. That out of the bad, there's a bit of good."

Like a bucket of water had splashed over my head, every wary vibe I'd had about Ollie vanished. With those few words, he'd just given me a peek into his soul, and I knew then without a shadow of a doubt that there wasn't a malicious or vengeful inch of him. *He's one of the rare good ones, isn't he? And he saved my life. Holy shit, he* saved *me*. How did you pay someone back for that? Was it even possible?

There was a sting behind my eyes and in my chest. "Thank you. For helping me just now and for...you know." *Saving my life.*

Ollie's gaze drifted to mine. "You're welcome."

An odd thought occurred to me then. "No wonder you came to see me in the hospital. Those flowers you brought...they were from you, weren't they?"

"Uh..." His face flushed darker than his hair. "Well, I knew you'd had another surgery, so..."

"But then I woke up and had no idea you were the one who saved me. Shit. I'm sorry." I gripped the back of my neck as my head fell back against the headrest. "I feel like I've lost so much."

"What makes you say that?"

"Until a few minutes ago, I couldn't remember my accident, and I think that's what I saw just now. I felt like I was there. And then there's this chunk of time that's missing between that day and the day of my surgery. And I can't explain it, I don't know what it is, but there's something in my gut that tells me that I have to keep digging."

Ollie sat up straighter. "Digging for what?"

"I don't know, whatever it is. I know that makes no sense. But have you ever had that feeling like you're forgetting something and everyone around you thinks you're crazy?"

He stared at me for a long moment and then nodded.

With a sigh, I massaged my temples with my thumbs. "I don't even know why I'm telling you all of this." It was strange how easy I found him to talk to, especially considering I hadn't spoken to many of my closest friends in so long. But I couldn't seem to shut myself up, and he was a good listener. *Maybe Mom's right. I do need a friend outside of my therapist.* "You're a saint, Ollie. I bet you had no idea you'd signed up for this when you offered me a ride."

"You seem like you needed to get it out."

"It's your fault you're easy to talk to."

A smile split his lips. "I'll take that as a compliment. You can talk to me anytime."

There it was. That strange niggling in my stomach. Shit, maybe I was hungry. Glancing at the time on the radio, I realized half an hour had already gone by.

"I think I've embarrassed myself enough for one day. I should probably go home," I said.

"Um, about that. Getting you home might be a problem."

"Why?"

"Is there a back entrance to your complex?"

"No, just the main one."

"Well, the accident happened right in front of your street, so it's blocked off right now. It'll take a little while before they can get the road cleared, so I won't be able to get you home until then. Are you hungry? Do you wanna go grab some lunch while we wait?"

I looked out at where we were and silently cursed. The rain pounded the car so heavily that Ollie's windshield wipers were working overtime and you could barely see anything ahead. Ugh, great. I was not looking forward to what I'd have to do next.

"How about you drive me up as close as you can and I can walk the rest of the way?"

"Uh, Reid?" Ollie pointed up at the car ceiling and we listened for a moment. "Pretty sure that's hail beating my car to shit right now. So unless you want a concussion, I wouldn't advise walking. Not to mention you'd have to pass the scene, and after the attack you had, I'm guessing you don't want to do that."

Shit, he was right. Okay, plan B. "My parents live in Bridgewood on Leigh Street. You can take me there."

"You got it."

He put the car in drive and eased back out onto the main road.

"It's not that I can't drive," I said to break up the quiet, suddenly feeling like a teenager who had to get his parents to come pick him up and drop him off. "I just haven't been able to bring myself to do it again yet."

"That's okay." No judgment, no questions. Just "okay." Still, I felt the need to explain myself so this guy didn't think badly of me for whatever reason. But before I could do that, Ollie said, "You'll do it when you're ready." He glanced over at me. "You've been through a lot, Reid. Give yourself a break."

Give myself a break? That was something I wasn't sure I could do.

Silence fell between us again, only this time it wasn't awkward. I pointed out how to get to my parents' house, and a few minutes later, he pulled into the driveway.

"You know," he said, rubbing his chin again, "I actually don't live far from here."

"You don't?"

"Nope. I'm on the other side of the lake off Wheeler Street."

"You weren't kidding. That is close."

"Mhmm. So if you're ever in the area, you should stop by. Since you like to walk"—he shrugged—"I do laps around the lake almost every day. You can join me if you want. We can talk. Not talk. Whatever."

"You're making that offer even though you've seen firsthand that I'm a mess?"

Ollie grinned. "Yeah, you're kind of a mess."

"Hey, you're not supposed to agree."

With a laugh, he held up his hand. "What I meant to say is we're all a little fucked up. That's not a deal breaker among friends."

Friends...hell, maybe I could use a friend. And it wouldn't be a bad idea to have one who seemed to keep paper bags around.

"Give me your number; maybe I'll call you next time I come over this way," I said.

He opened the glove compartment and took out a pen and a napkin, and it didn't escape my notice the way his hands shook as he wrote down his number. Then again, he did have the air on high and was still sporting his wet clothes. I reached over and turned down the AC so he wouldn't freeze to death.

When he handed me the paper, I shoved it in my wallet to keep it from getting drenched.

"Thanks again for the ride, Ollie. And for...well, all of it. You're a good man to have around."

"No problem at all. Take care, Reid."

Take care, Reid... Those words brought on déjà vu as I stepped out of the car and made a run for the porch. I turned and waved before heading inside, and Ollie flashed his lights in goodbye.

There was something innately comforting about that guy, which was odd considering his dominating size. Maybe I could use someone like that in my life.

CHAPTER SIX

OLLIE

NO ONE WAS more shocked than I was when Reid actually called a few days later. I'd been positive our next interaction would be when I attended his class on Sunday, but the guy had more guts than I'd given him credit for. I'd just gotten out of the shower after a low-key workday, getting ready to head downtown for dinner and beers with Mike and Deb, when my cell buzzed.

"Hi, this is Reid. You know, the one who spazzed in your car the other day? I told you I'd call when I was over your way, and... well, I'm over your way," he said when I answered.

I was glad in that moment that he wasn't standing right in front of me, because the smile that took over my whole face then would've given away my true feelings for sure.

"I'm glad you did," I said.

"Yeah?"

"Yeah."

"Well...are you busy right now?"

"Actually, I was on my way out."

"Oh." The disappointment in his voice stirred something

inside me, bringing that damn flicker of hope back to full flame. "Maybe next time, then."

"If you don't mind a couple of loudmouth friends of mine giving you an inquisition over drinks, how would you feel about joining us?"

"Join you and your friends? Um..."

"No pressure. Mike can be a bit of a handful, though Deb's not much better, but they're entertaining as hell and they'll love you."

"I don't know that your friends would be okay with you bringing some weirdo stranger around. I can just give you a call next time I'm in the neighborhood."

"Reid?"

"Yeah?"

"You haven't met weird until you've met these two."

"Is that supposed to convince me to go?" he said, laughing.

"I think it means you need to see them for yourself to believe it. Then maybe you'll realize how normal you are."

"I seriously doubt that, but it sounds like an interesting challenge."

Say yes. Say yes. I was trying not to beg here.

"Are you sure they'll be okay with me tagging along?"

"Are you kidding? They'll be so grateful to have someone else to talk to besides me that they'll probably kick me out of the group." When he laughed again, I said, "Come on. It'll do you some good to get out and meet a few people, and the food's damn good too. Whaddya say?"

Reid laughed. "I say you put up a good argument. I think you convinced me, if only to meet the weirdos."

"Perfect. I'll pick you up in ten."

"See you then."

"YOU'RE SHITTIN' ME," Mike shouted from where we sat at a high-top at Wilder's, a restaurant-slash-bar downtown. I'd gotten a couple of beer pitchers for the table, and he'd been busy pouring himself a glass when I broke the news that Reid had come with me. Good timing for him to be washing his hands when double trouble arrived.

"Keep your damn voice down," I said.

"Hell no I'm not keeping my voice down. He's here?"

"Yes, so please don't embarrass me. Jesus." I took a sip of my beer. "I'm regretting this already."

"No, this is great," he said, then raised his hand to get the waiter's attention. "We need shots over here. Shit-ton of shots."

"That is the last thing we need."

"Ollie's right," Deb said, as she sidled up against her husband and then winked at me. "We should wait until Reid comes back."

I shook my head. "You're just as bad of an influence as he is, you know that?"

With a coy grin, she put her hand on her hip and cocked it to the side. "You didn't think Mike wore the pants in this relationship, did you?"

No, I knew for a fact that Deb ran that household. She might only be five two in heels, but she could shame a man my size with her voice. I never could understand how such a small woman could have such a loud set of lungs, but that little blond spitfire always surprised me.

"Before he gets back, please remember that he has no idea who you are and he barely knows me. Treat him like you would someone you don't know," I said.

"Treat him like a stranger. Got it," Deb said, and then a big smile lit up her face as her eyes went over my shoulder. "Oh my God!" She squealed over the music and ran over to attack Reid as he approached by throwing her arms around him. "You must be Reid. It's so good to meet you."

Reid looked at me with raised brows, and I groaned. Leave it to Deb to think greeting a stranger meant with a tackle hug.

"She does it to everyone," Mike said as he reached out to shake Reid's hand. "I'm Mike, Ollie's better half on the job, and I claim the spider monkey clinging to you. Sometimes."

Deb finally let go of Reid and swatted her husband.

"Oh, hi," Reid said. "You're a paramedic too?"

"I prefer the term Lord of Big Bertha, but I guess that works."

Reid furrowed his brow and looked at me. "Big Bertha?"

"That's what we call our ambulance," I said. "Though if he's the lord, I don't know what that makes me."

"My bitch?" Mike suggested.

"Ohhh, he is gonna squash you like a bug, babe. How about you go grab us those shots?" Deb slapped Mike on the ass and sent him off to the bar before turning back to us. "So, Reid," Deb said, batting her lashes, "Ollie tells us he assaulted your ears in your class the other day."

Reid looked over at me and grinned. "Did he?"

"I don't recall using the word 'assault,' Deb," I said. "Thanks for that."

"I've heard you do karaoke, Ollie." Deb cut her eyes at Reid. "Don't ever encourage him to sing Queen. As a matter of fact, don't encourage him to sing at all. Trust me."

"That bad, huh?" Reid said, amusement twitching his lips.

Deb nodded. "I still wake up having nightmares about it."

"Oh please," I said. "Anyone's *that bad* after a few pitchers of margaritas."

"Instead of 'fandango,' you sang, 'Will you do the damn tango?'"

"An artistic choice."

"I dunno, Ollie," Reid said. "Anyone who destroys a Freddie Mercury song shouldn't be allowed anywhere near a microphone. Or a piano."

Pretending to look at my watch, I said, "And on that note from the gang-up police, I think it's time for me to go."

"Oh stay." Deb grabbed my shirt when I tried to walk off. "Let us embarrass you until Mike gets back. Then we can rag on him."

"Rag on me for what?" Mike said, coming up behind her with a tray of shots.

"Uh, you know we have to work tomorrow, right?" I said.

"Live a little, my man. This is why God gave you a strong liver and created Uber." He passed a couple of shots to each of us, and I sniffed at the liquor. Fuck—tequila. Yeah, I'd only be having one of those tonight.

"So what'll it be, huh?" Mike waggled his brows at me, and I knew that meant I needed to come up with a toast quickly before something vile spewed from his mouth.

"To new friends," I said, lifting my shot glass, and Mike rolled his eyes and mouthed, *You're so lame*. Mike and Deb on tequila was not gonna be a great first impression for Reid. Lord help us all.

"To new friends," they said, and we clinked glasses before tossing back the liquid—no salt or lemon for this crowd.

"Ugh. Does anyone actually *like* the taste of tequila?" I shuddered and set my empty glass on the tray. "Why can't we do something that tastes good?"

"Aww," Mike said, poking out his bottom lip like a pouty child would. "Does Ollie need a little lemon drop? Maybe you'd like a Sex on the Beach while you're at it. Something with a pink umbrella."

"Hey, those sound good to me," Reid piped up. God, he looked good tonight. He did every time I saw him, but it was like seeing him for the first time all over again. He wore tan slacks and a fitted black polo shirt that made his dark eyes and hair seem even more striking, and I thought again, for maybe the millionth time, how drop-dead gorgeous he was.

"You don't have to take his side just because he brought you here. We'll make sure you have a way home." Mike winked as he chased down another shot with his beer.

"Anyway," Deb said, tossing her hair over her shoulder and focusing her attention back on Reid. "You are just too handsome for words. You seeing anyone?"

Reid blinked. "Uh—"

"Don't answer that," I said, topping his beer off when I noticed it was low. I didn't need her help pushing his buttons, *thankyouverymuch*.

Deb glared my way. "Is your name Reid? I didn't think so." Then the tight line of her lips transformed back into a smile. "So?"

Reid took a long sip before answering, and when he did, his cheeks flushed. "No, I'm not seeing anyone. Life's been a little crazy lately for that."

"I understand," she said. "That's the excuse Ollie tries to give every time we set him up with someone too."

"Oh... Does that happen a lot?" Reid asked.

Mike interjected, "No, because our friend here thinks it's funny to ditch us and not show up."

"Hey," I said, holding up my hand. "It's not that I don't appreciate that you want me as gaggingly happy as you two, but I don't need your help. And I definitely don't want to sit through dinner on a blind date while you watch."

"Hell no. No blind dates. It may be the best intentions of friends and all, but those dates never end well," Reid said. "I swore them off years ago."

"So you'd rather date someone you're already friendly with, then?" Deb said, and I didn't miss the way she looked pointedly at me while she asked.

You better fucking stop, I tried to convey with my narrowed eyes, but she just smirked and bit down on a loaded nacho.

"I guess I haven't really thought about it," Reid admitted.

"Hmm. And what about you, Ollie?" she said. "Have you thought much about it?"

I pushed my second shot her way. "Drink up and stay out of my love life, please, Deb."

Mike snorted. "Fat chance of that happening. She wouldn't know what to do with herself if she couldn't interfere."

"I heard that."

With a laugh, Reid dug into the nachos and popped one into his mouth. When he finished chewing, he pointed at Mike and Deb. "So what about you two? You seem perfect for each other. How'd you meet?"

"Yeah, guys," I said, and sipped my drink. "Why don't you tell him?"

As Deb fficked me off and then launched into the story about how she'd accidentally knocked Mike unconscious with a wayward swing of her tennis racket in college, I couldn't help but think about how this meeting between Reid and my closest friends had finally taken place, months after we'd made plans. Plans we never got to follow through on because I'd taken Reid to the emergency room that week instead. So to see the three of them all together around the same table, laughing and ribbing each other as if they'd known each other for years...well, it had a warm and fuzzy feeling humming through my veins. Even if Reid never regained his memory, even if he never looked at me with eyes of lust or more, then I thought maybe, just maybe, this would be enough. I wasn't sure how my heart would feel about that decision, but my head was ruling matters now, and it said I needed to suck it up and be grateful. Reid was here, he was alive, and he'd chosen to spend tonight with me. That was a win.

Life had a funny way of trying to come full circle, didn't it?

A burst of laughter came out of all three of them, and as I looked up to see what I'd missed, a familiar gaze caught my eye.

Holland Kennedy had spiked white-blond hair, a slim build, and had been a friend with benefits on my short list for a long time, but it'd been over a year since I'd seen him, or seen his number pop up on my phone.

But he sure saw me now, his crooked smile widening as he started in my direction.

Oh fuck. Not now. Not here.

There was no way I wanted a reunion in front of Reid, even if all we'd ever be was platonic, so I quickly excused myself from the table before Holland could make his approach...and turn it all to shit.

CHAPTER SEVEN

REID

WHEN OLLIE TOLD us he'd be right back, I figured he was going to the restroom or maybe the bar for more food or drinks. What I didn't expect was that he'd walk straight over to a surfer-looking guy, who greeted him with a hug and a kiss on the cheek.

Whatever Deb had been saying faded into the background as I zeroed in on their interaction. The guy rubbed Ollie's spine before Ollie broke off the embrace and took a step back. But as the two continued to converse, the other guy touched Ollie's arm and leaned back into him to whisper something in his ear. The way the blond smiled at him and invaded his personal space made me think they'd been intimate with each other at some point. Or maybe even now. Ollie had said he was single, but maybe that didn't refer to hookups.

I pushed my beer away as my stomach began to churn, and when the guy's hand slid up Ollie's arm again, a different scene sprang to my mind—one at a bowling alley with a guy in a red shirt, staring at Ollie in a way that made me want to give them privacy, but also made my blood heat.

"I hope you don't mind, but I noticed you were giving your friend pointers, and I thought...maybe you could help me as well?" red shirt guy said, ignoring me completely as he licked his lips and smiled at Ollie.

"Actually, I'm a little busy—" Ollie said from where he stood beside me and had been showing me the right technique for keeping my bowling ball out of the gutter.

"That's okay. I'm a quick learner." He gave Ollie a long once-over. "It won't take long."

"I don't think—"

"You should go." The words came out of my mouth automatically, even though that was the last thing I wanted. "It's selfish to keep you all to myself when you could be helping someone else."

"Reid?"

My eyes snapped up to Ollie's from where I'd apparently been staring off into space while lost in whatever that had been. That couldn't have been a memory. I'd never been at a bowling alley with Ollie. Had I drifted off to sleep standing up or something?

I shook my head, erasing the images from my mind. "I'm sorry, what did you say?"

"Everything okay?" Ollie asked, coming around the table to stand beside me. When I looked up, Deb and Mike had resumed their conversation, but I could see them peeking over to see what was going on.

Way to make a scene by daydreaming, Reid.

"Everything's good. Maybe need to lay off the drinks and eat something," I said, and reached for another nacho.

"Yeah, of course, let's go ahead and order. Did you decide what you want already?"

"Hmm. What's good?"

Ollie flipped open a menu, and we both scanned over it. "Their chicken enchiladas are amazing, but I gotta say, their fish tacos bring it home for me."

Something flickered on the edges of my mind. "Tacos?"

"Yeah. You like tacos, right?"

"With homemade seasoning," I murmured. *A mixing bowl. Spices spread out along the counter, and Ollie pouring them one at a time as he smiled at...me?*

"Well, I don't know how homemade the seasoning is here, but it gets the job done. You'll have to come over the next time I make some and try it out."

My forehead creased, and I rubbed it with my thumb. "You make your own?"

"It's the only way."

"Right." I knew that. How did I know that?

"So what do you think?" Ollie said. "Wanna try 'em out?"

I could hear him talking, but all my mind could seem to focus on was the image of Ollie mixing spices. *Get it together before he decides to cut the night short and take you home.* "Sure. Fish tacos sound great."

And they were. Fresh and perfectly flaky with some kind of creamy sauce that had me licking my fingers. When I moaned while savoring my last bite, Ollie chuckled.

"Doesn't look like you enjoyed those at all. I really should give better recommendations," he said.

"Yes, terrible choice. Absolutely hated them." I grinned and sucked a bit of sauce from my finger, and Ollie's eyes dropped down to my mouth. But then he quickly looked away, over to where Mike and Deb two-stepped on the dance floor. Or at least that was what I thought they were supposed to be doing. Mike seemed to be making up a few moves, complete with hip thrusts that had Deb laughing her ass off.

"Your friends are pretty interesting," I said.

"That's a nice way to put it."

"I mean that in a good way. You're lucky to have people who care about you the way they obviously do."

"You think?"

"Yeah. They seem protective in that way that says they'll kick the ass of anyone who messes with you. And they welcomed me tonight with no hesitation, not even knowing anything about me other than you invited me. Not to mention they're hilarious."

"Oh God. Please don't say any of this to Mike. It's already hard enough to get his ego through the door."

I let out a laugh, because I had no doubt that was true, or at least half true. Mike seemed to be in on the joke. "Did you guys meet at work?"

"No, actually. We met before that." He stopped and gripped the back of his neck as his cheeks turned pink. "I, uh, dated Deb's cousin, so I'd met them at some dinner or...something."

"Oh. So you could've been family, huh?"

"Well, they're the closest thing I have to family, so yeah. I guess you could say I got them in the breakup."

The closest thing to family? "You don't have brothers or sisters? Family nearby?"

He shook his head. "I'm an only child. My parents passed away when I was seventeen, and I've been on my own ever since."

Holy shit. For some reason, I wasn't all that surprised at his words, but I *was* surprised at how they affected me. An intense wave of sympathy and crushing sadness filled my chest as I realized this man beside me, who I'd thought was so sure of himself when I met him, was all alone in the world, save for Mike and

Deb. Or did he have anyone else? Aunts, uncles, cousins? Grandparents? I got the feeling if I asked him, he'd tell me no, because wouldn't they have taken him in when his parents passed? And again I felt the twinge of guilt for how I'd treated my own parents over the last few weeks.

As if reading my thoughts, Ollie said, "It's okay. I'm not a sob story, I promise." Then he nudged me, trying to lighten the mood, but something else had popped into my brain, something that came out of nowhere but I knew to be true, though I didn't know how.

"They died in a car accident, didn't they? Your parents?"

Ollie's brows shot up. "Good guess."

But it wasn't a guess. At least, I didn't think it was. Shit. Had my accident caused me to become clairvoyant or something? First the bowling guy, then the taco seasoning, and now this? "Yeah," I said, swallowing. "Lucky guess."

As I looked over to where Mike and Deb were slow-dancing in the middle of the crowded floor, another pair of eyes nearby caught my attention. Blond surfer guy was staring at Ollie...or maybe he was staring between the two of us, I couldn't tell, and something about the way he looked in our direction made me want to hit him—a reaction that surprised the shit out of me, considering I wasn't usually a violent person and I didn't know him from Adam. But when he didn't look away, I finally asked Ollie who he was—not that it was any of my business.

Ollie looked over in the guy's direction. "Who, Holland over there? He's just someone I used to hang out with."

Holland? What kind of a name is Holland? "Used to?"

"Yeah, I haven't seen him in a while."

"Why not?"

"Been busy."

"But you used to date?"

He paused lifting his drink to his lips. "I wouldn't call it that," he said, and then finished off the iced water he'd switched to just as Mike and Deb came back to the table, and that was the end of that. I didn't even know why I cared, but it bothered me that surfer guy had been anywhere near him. From his actions in the car the other day to tonight, Ollie seemed like too good of a guy to attach himself to someone slimy like that.

Oh please. I wanted to roll my eyes at myself. *He's probably a perfectly decent guy.* Then, like a devil was sitting on my shoulder, I thought, *Yeah, a perfectly decent guy who's been in Ollie's pants.*

I scrubbed a hand over my face. What the hell? It wasn't like I gave a shit who anyone else dated, especially not some guy I'd just met. Emphasis on *guy*.

God, I was officially losing it.

And on top of that, I was suddenly hyperaware of where Ollie was at all times. Every time he'd accidentally brush against my arm as he laughed at something Mike said, or when he'd reach across me to refill drinks, it felt like a shock of static. I wondered if he even felt it on his end, because he didn't jerk away like I did when it happened.

One thing that stood out to me—Ollie smiled a lot, a genuine, wide grin that lit up his face. Sitting so close, I even noticed the small scar along the edge of his jaw, which I'd never seen before because it was mostly hidden by the scruff he kept trimmed down short, but it was there. I wondered how he'd gotten it.

"Do I have something on my face?" he asked, wiping his beard as he caught me staring.

"Uh, yeah, some sauce or something right there," I lied, pointing to a spot on my chin, and he swept away the imaginary crumb.

"Did I get it?"

Damn, he had piercing eyes, so light green tonight that they almost glowed. They were the kind that forced you to spill all your secrets, but promised to keep them safe and hidden.

"Yeah," I said, my voice coming out gravelly, and I cleared my throat. "Yeah, you got it."

I turned my attention back to Mike and Deb, and the rest of the night passed with them lobbing insults not only at Ollie, but also at each other and sometimes even me, which, I had a feeling, meant they didn't mind me crashing their party tonight. A couple of hours later, my stomach muscles ached from laughing so hard, and it made me hope this wasn't the last time I'd score an invite out with the three of them. I hadn't realized how desperately I'd been missing out on having people in my life to go out with or laugh with for a couple of hours. To make me feel somewhat human again, even if I wasn't sure that I'd ever get my life back to normal. Or my old sense of normal, anyway.

"All right, all right, all right," Mike bellowed, doing his best Matthew McConaughey impersonation, though it was a bit slurred. "What time is it?" He blinked down at his watch. "Holy shit. Woman, why you make me stay out so late?"

Deb winked at me. "It's Reid's fault. He kept making you do his tequila shots."

"Ohh, that asshole," Mike said, narrowing his eyes at me. "Next time, you hold your own damn liquor. I'm not a storage closet."

"I think he means human garbage disposal," she whispered loudly.

"That's what I said." Mike rounded the table and gave Ollie a hug. Or fell into him, rather.

"I'll drop you guys off," Ollie said, as Mike then gave me a hug.

"Thanks, but I already confirmed an Uber." Deb lifted her phone to show us the little black car moving toward Wilder's, and then she came over to me, lifting up on her tiptoes to smack a kiss to my cheek. "You're gonna come hang out with us again soon, right? You have to. Don't let Ollie keep you away." Then she turned and pointed a stern finger in Ollie's direction. "You hear me, Olls? You make him come back."

"I'll be sure to drag him out against his will if he even thinks about protesting," Ollie agreed.

That seemed to appease Deb, because she said, "Good boy," and then patted my jaw before Mike put his arm around her shoulder.

"The chariot awaits, my lady," he said, leading her away, and then, over his shoulder, he pointed at me. "Don't think you're getting out of karaoke next week."

"I'll make sure to bring my cotton balls for Ollie's performance," I said.

"Ohhh shit!" Mike said, as the three of them went slack-jawed. "He went there. Ollie, he went there, and I think I'm in love. Deb, I'm leaving you, sorry." Mike stumbled back in my direction, and Deb laughed and pulled him back.

"You stupid ass. He'd make you sleep outside," she said as his arm went back around her shoulders, and then she winked at us. "Later, guys."

"Bye, Deb. Make sure his alarm is set," Ollie said, and when he faced me again, he shook his head. "Well. You survived."

I checked over my arms and legs. "No battle wounds that I can see. They weren't too scary."

"No? I'll make sure they bring it next time."

So there would be a next time... "Looking forward to it," I said—and meant it.

"Good. You about ready to head out?"

"Yeah, gimme five minutes?"

"Sure."

I walked down the narrow hallway toward the one-stall bathrooms, but when the door was locked, I leaned against the wall to wait. A minute later, the door opened, and out came surfer guy—Holland, Ollie had called him. *Stupid name*—and when he saw me, he stopped and gave me a long once-over, letting the door shut behind him.

"No wonder Ollie wasn't up for getting together later," he said, a lazy smile tipping his lips.

"Excuse me?"

His eyes met mine and he smirked. "I meant that as a compliment. You're sexy as hell."

Okay, that wasn't what I'd been expecting. "Uh...thanks."

"You're welcome," he said, and then mimicked my pose, leaning against the wall and crossing his arms. "You know, I hadn't realized Ollie was seeing anyone, but I guess you two are serious, huh?"

"No, sorry. I think you're mistaking me for someone else."

The guy laughed, his pearly whites flashing in the dim light. "Nah, I'd never forget a face, especially one as handsome as yours. You've been dating since, what, February? I saw you guys at Fisherman's Grill one night, but I was on a date of my own, so I didn't come say hello."

My face burned as I stepped back. "You've got the wrong guy. We just met."

"Sure you did, sweet pea," he said, laughing again. "I wouldn't be ashamed of claiming that man as mine. You let me know if you decide to give him up. Or vice versa." With a wink, he pushed off the wall and brushed past me, and it wasn't until I reached for the door handle that I realized my hands were shaking.

What the hell was that? Why would he think I was with Ollie back in February, for God's sake? Do I have a twin I don't know about?

I quickly finished and met Ollie back at the table, where he was stacking up the glasses on the table for the wait staff to have an easy cleanup. There was a signed copy of a bill next to him, and I scanned the table for mine.

"Did they forget to print mine out?" I asked.

"Oh, don't worry about it. I got it tonight." Ollie shoved a copy in his back pocket and inclined his head toward the front door. "You ready?"

With my mind still on my bathroom encounter, I nodded absently and followed him out to the parking lot. I wasn't sure how to bring up what Holland had said back there, or why it bothered me so much when he'd obviously gotten the wrong person, but after a night of strange images and flashes berating my brain, I was feeling more than a little confused and overwhelmed. I just needed to sleep it off, right? Right. Maybe I'd just gotten overstimulated or something. Like a fucking cat. Or maybe alcohol had screwed with my head. Then I thought back to the way Ollie had looked at my mouth for the briefest of moments and that he'd paid for me tonight, and I wasn't sure what to think anymore. Maybe I'd had this whole night wrong.

Ollie must've caught on to my sudden change in mood, because he said, "Are you sure Mike and Deb didn't scare you off? I know they're a bit of a handful, and on tequila, it's amped up about a hundred percent."

"No, your friends are great. I really like them a lot. Wild, but great."

"Whew. You got quiet for a minute there, so I wasn't sure."

I hadn't planned to say anything, really I hadn't, but the words came blurting out before I could stop them. "This wasn't a date, you know."

He gave me a strange look. "Yeah, I know."

"Then why did you pay for me?"

"I paid for Mike and Deb's food too. Friends do that sometimes. That a problem?"

"You didn't have to do that."

"I'm aware. But I wanted to. I invited you out. And it's the least I can do for subjecting you to Mike's mouth all night."

"Oh. Well...thank you."

"You're welcome." I could sense him looking over at me, but I wouldn't meet his eyes. "Is there something else wrong?"

"No."

"Reid, I can feel the tension coming off you in waves. Did you not have a good time tonight?"

"I did."

"So...?"

I had a feeling he wasn't gonna let it go until I told him what was really bothering me, and even though it was an irrational thing to say, I found the words coming out anyway as I spun around to face him. "Look, I'm not gay."

Ollie raised an eyebrow. "I know."

"Do you? Because it doesn't feel that way."

He stopped walking. "What are you talking about?"

"I'm saying is this some kind of game you have with your friends? Try to turn the straight guy?" My anger and confusion combined and kept tumbling out, and I couldn't make it stop.

"*Excuse* me?"

"Because if it is, you're barking up the wrong tree."

"Whoa," he said, holding up his hands. "When have I *ever* given you the impression tonight that I was hitting on you? Besides paying the bill, which was not a big deal."

"The guy back there? The one you hugged? He said he saw me with you one night at Fisherman's Grill before."

Ollie went to reply, stopped short, and stared at me. "He said what?"

"Why would he think he saw me with you? I know I've never been there with you, so what's the deal, huh? Do I look like someone you used to date? Is that why you invited me out tonight?"

Even with just the lights of the restaurant to illuminate us, I could see that his face had gone ghostly white, and his body was so still that I wasn't sure if he was still breathing. When he spoke again, his voice strained barely above a whisper. "No. I didn't invite you out because you look like someone I dated. I don't know why Holland would tell you that. I'm sorry if he made you uncomfortable."

My mouth clamped shut, and I scrubbed a hand over my face. "No, I'm sorry. That was an asshole thing to say. I don't even know why I said it."

Ollie stared at me for a long minute, like he was trying to figure out who the hell had taken over my personality, and quite frankly, I was wondering the same thing. Why had I felt the need to bring any of that up? I'd never cared what anyone thought of me before, and it wasn't like I was bothered over Ollie being gay, or anyone thinking I was, for that matter.

Ollie's jaw ticked as he unlocked the car, and once we were both inside, he said, "You may find this hard to believe, but gay people have platonic friends too. Not everyone is a sexual target."

"I know that," I said in a quiet voice. "I didn't mean it."

"Do you have a habit of saying things you don't mean?"

"Lately I seem to."

"And why is that?"

"I'm not sure."

"Automatic defensive reflex, maybe?" he said.

"Yeah. Maybe."

He sighed and stared out the window. "Look, Reid. I know you've got a lot going on right now. There's probably a lot you don't understand, stuff you're still figuring out, but do me a favor. Don't take it out on the people trying to help you."

His words struck a chord with me, sending a pang through my chest. "I apologize. I think this was a mistake."

"What, coming out tonight?"

"I'm just a little...fucked up right now." Yeah, that wasn't even the half of it. I was being ridiculous. He knew it, I knew it, and I couldn't for the life of me understand why. All I knew was that I was entirely too pissed off about that guy Holland, and I was paying way too much attention to Ollie's mouth, the way he had mine earlier. But I'd meant what I said: I wasn't gay. Not that I hadn't noticed Ollie when we'd get our coffee every morning at Joe's, but how could you help but notice him? He was a big guy. But now I wasn't so sure that was the only reason.

What the hell is happening to me?

It was dead silent the entire drive to my apartment, one of those uncomfortable silences where you knew you needed to fill it with apologies or explanations, but the words wouldn't come out. I couldn't unravel the conflict and chaos warring inside of me. On one hand, I'd enjoyed the night more than I'd ever expected to, and it had more to do with the man beside me than Mike and Deb's jokes. There was something inherently kind about Ollie, even now, as he patiently deflected the jabs I'd hurled his way. It made me wonder why he bothered with me, and if he ever would again. I wouldn't blame him for cutting ties and running, though for some inexplicable reason, the thought of never seeing him again sent a blast of panic through me.

Once we were in my neighborhood, Ollie circled around until he found an open parking space, but he didn't shut off the car.

"For the record, I'm not sorry you came out tonight," he said, and then looked over at me. "I'm only sorry you feel it was a mistake."

With my hand on the door handle, I opened my mouth to apologize, but the words dissolved on my tongue with one look at the sincerity on his face. The truth was that the guy scared me—not in a boogie man kind of way, but in a way that had me questioning everything I thought I knew about myself. More than anything, I hated that I'd disappointed him, but I had a feeling any apology I gave tonight would be tossed aside, and so I simply thanked him for letting me tag along and headed upstairs to my empty apartment—alone and more miserable than I had been in a long time.

CHAPTER EIGHT

REID

I WAS A zombie the next day and all through dinner with my folks that evening. I replayed the night over and over again in my head, and I still couldn't believe how badly I'd acted last night. Lashing out at Ollie was the final straw that told me I needed to figure my shit out. He'd been nothing but good to me from day one, and I'd shown my ass. It wasn't like me at all, and I had no excuse. None. But even though my fingers itched to pull out my phone and call him to apologize, I had another problem.

The chair across from me was now empty, Anna having discreetly disappeared from the table at some point. The hug she'd given me the other day was apparently a distant memory, since she was back to avoiding me and dipping out early whenever I was around.

It seemed like a Reid apology tour was in order, because I was done pissing off the people around me. I had issues I needed to work through, and I couldn't begin to do that if I didn't confront the problems I knew I could fix. Starting with my sister.

After excusing myself from the table, I looked in her room, but when I didn't see her, I headed for the back door. I knew

Anna was having a hard time coming to terms with the last few months just as I was, and I needed her just as much as she needed me. Even with the age difference, we'd been close, and I wanted to mend the rift between us. I knew she missed me, but she didn't want to admit it. We needed to talk, and I knew just where to find her.

The sun still shone brightly in the sky as I crossed the sidewalk behind my parents' house and headed down the grassy bank to where Anna stood tossing bits of leftover dinner rolls to the ducks.

"Hey, Banana."

She flinched at my voice but didn't turn around. "I thought you would've left already."

"No. Why? Do you want me to leave?"

She shrugged her delicate shoulders and then threw another piece of the roll even farther out.

I was determined to heal our relationship, somehow, someway. But she wasn't making it easy by keeping herself closed off. *Hey, whaddya know, sort of like you, huh, asshole?*

"Do you mind if we talk?" I asked as I came up beside her. She was almost as tall as me now, and lanky, though she was no athlete. She was more into books and poetry and always had been.

Anna shrugged again, and I dropped down to the grass to make myself comfortable.

"Do you remember when Mom and Dad took us to that hidden waterfall that one time? Not Valentine Falls, the other one." When she didn't answer, I continued. "You didn't know how to swim very well yet, so you stayed on the rocks, climbing over them like they were a jungle gym. Then out of nowhere that big-ass bird...what was it, a hawk? It swooped down close to you and scared you to death. I remember seeing it happen and watching as you lost your balance and hit your head on those rocks."

Anna wiped off her hands and sat down beside me, still not looking my way.

"You scared me to death that day. Practically gave Mom and Dad a heart attack, too. You were out cold for a minute, and when you came to, we cut the day short."

"What does that have to do with anything?" she said.

"Don't you see? The same thing could've easily happened to you that happened to me. We both got knocked unconscious, but it wasn't your fault that you fell any more than it was my fault that a truck ran a red light. What if you'd woken up and didn't know who I was either?"

She stared straight ahead, but I could see her eyes welling.

"I would've moved mountains, sung bad karaoke, whipped out all the family photo albums until you were sick of looking at my face until you remembered who I was. Because you're my sister, my banana, and I'm your brother. I will always love you. No matter what."

A tear fell down her cheek, and she brushed it away.

"It would just take you a little longer to realize it, is all."

"So you're saying it's my fault I haven't tried hard enough?"

"No. God no. I just don't want you to be scared of me. I want you to know that I'm here. I'm not going anywhere. But I won't lie to you—I'm a little lost right now. I hate that there are things I can't remember, and sometimes I can't tell if the things that pop into my head are memories or dreams or if I'm hallucinating. So if you see me drifting off into space with a confused look on my face, I'm gonna need you to bring me back down to earth."

"How do I do that?"

"I'm sure you'll think of something."

"Maybe get Dad to hold you down while I tickle your feet?"

"You're evil," I said, shaking my head. "But if that works, I'll take it."

"But what if it happens again?" Her voice cracked, and when I put my arm around her, pulling her closer, she didn't put up a protest.

"There's probably a point zero zero zero one percent chance it could happen a third time, but God knows if it did, then I'd ask you all to commit me to a psych ward and leave me there. By then I'd be totally confused with reality."

She let out a little chuckle and sniffed.

"I understand not wanting to open yourself up to getting hurt again. And I know I hurt you involuntarily. I get that. But you're my sister, the only one I've got in this world, and I love you. I don't want you to be scared of me or avoid me. I want us to spend time together again. Go get lost in old bookstores, or go see a movie or get ice cream."

"Does this mean I'd get to drive?"

"Oh shit. I'm not sure I'm ready for that." When she sat up and punched me in the arm, I said, "I was kidding. I'll think about it. For now, there's Uber or Mom and Dad."

She smiled and then peered up at me. "Reid?"

"Yeah?"

"I'm really sorry." Dropping her gaze, she began to pull strands of grass out of the ground one at a time. "It was so hard when you woke up from the coma. You treated me like a little sister—"

"You *are* my little sister."

"Yeah, but you've never treated me like one. We've always been…friends. And you were nice, but you didn't have much to do with me."

"I'm sorry, Anna. I wish I could take it back. It was confusing for the both of us, but you have to know I'd never want to hurt you."

"I do know that."

"You better. And we *are* friends. Which means if you're upset or need to talk, you come to me. Don't go trying to hide. I know where you live."

She snorted. "Dork."

"I know you are, but what am I?"

"A bigger dork."

"Am I forgiven, though?"

"Hmm," she said, pushing the dark brown strands that had escaped from her ponytail behind her ears. "Yeah, I guess. Since you asked nicely."

"Oh, gee, thanks. Tell you what, if I ever forget you again, you have my permission to slap me silly."

She laughed and rolled her eyes. "I can't slap someone with a brain injury, Reid, geez."

"You can if he's not thinking straight."

"Anna!" Mom called out from the back porch. "Don't think I've forgotten it's your turn to load the dishwasher."

I grinned and gave Anna a nudge. "You'd better get in there before she has a conniption fit and grounds you."

"Yeah, yeah." As we stood up and wiped the grass off our pants, she peered up at me. "Reid?"

"Hmm?"

"I love you."

"I love you too, Banana."

"Anna! I'm not gonna tell you again," Mom yelled.

"I'm coming," Anna called out, and I gave her one last squeeze before letting her go.

When she ran off, I felt a huge weight had lifted from my shoulders. I hadn't expected her forgiveness to come so readily, but maybe she'd wanted our relationship back as much as I did. I needed to plan some sibling time with her one day soon, but at least for the moment, it seemed like we might be okay.

Thank God.

I crossed her name off my mental checklist and moved down to the next name: Ollie. How to explain all my baggage to a new friend—if that was what we still were—and have him understand where I was coming from? I needed to figure out what to say to apologize for my behavior, so before I got around to calling him, I needed to clear my brain a bit.

A walk in the fresh evening air sounded like a good plan to me. The last thing I wanted to do was sound like a hot mess when I called. Although Ollie had already seen me have a panic attack followed by an attack on *him*, so chances were slim he'd even answer the phone for me at this point.

Man. It was a roaster of a day, a thousand degrees, give or take a few, and I was already regretting my decision to go for a walk. But since I was about halfway at that point, I figured I'd finish out the lap before heading inside.

As I reached for my phone in my pocket, my eyes landed on a house across the street and I stopped moving. There wasn't anything that stood out about the place for it to have gotten my attention. It was on the smaller side and had the same brick exterior as almost every other house in the neighborhood, only this one had a red door and green shutters.

But...that house. I *knew* that house, and not because I'd walked past it a hundred times before. There was a loose brick on the third porch step of that house.

Without knowing why, I found myself crossing the street. Maybe it was that I wanted to check that brick to make sure it was loose and I wasn't crazy. But what would it mean if it was? I couldn't recall ever coming here before. There would be no reason for me to know a detail like that.

Venturing across the yard, I noticed there was no car in the driveway, so at least the owner wouldn't see some crazy guy on their front lawn. *This is stupid,* I thought when I stood in front of the porch steps and debated whether to turn around and keep right on walking. But I'd come this far, and better to know I wasn't fully losing it...or not.

Stepping onto the first stair, I toed the edge of the bricks on the third step with my foot. On the right side, one of the bricks had darker edges surrounding it, and I bent over to wiggle it with my hand.

It didn't move.

Shit.

"Don't tell me the brick came loose again," came a voice from the driveway, and I whirled around to see Ollie getting out of his car, still dressed in his uniform of navy-blue pants and a matching button-down shirt that fit his muscular build like a glove.

"Ollie?" I rubbed my eyes, making sure I wasn't seeing things, but no. He was still there. "What are you doing here?" I said, as he opened his trunk and took out a few grocery bags. He easily slid them all up one arm and then shut the trunk with the other.

"What do you mean what am I doing here?" he said, giving me a funny look as he walked past me up the stairs. "It's my house. What are *you* doing here?"

His house? This was Ollie's house?

He tapped on the third step with his foot, right over the place with the darkened cracks. "Oh good. If that thing had come loose again, I would've chucked it into the lake."

Oh God. A wave of dizziness had me reaching for the rail to keep me upright.

My mind knew Ollie's house. But why...how? We'd just met, and I'd never been here before. But that detail was so strong, just like I knew if I walked up those steps, that it would lead into a hallway with dark blue walls and white trim before opening up into a living area and kitchen.

What the fuck is happening?

Ollie stood inside the unlocked doorway and looked down at me. "You comin'?"

Was I? I'd been about to call him anyway, but this revelation felt like my feet were being kicked out from under me. With shaky legs, I climbed up to where Ollie watched me with concern in his eyes.

"Everything okay?" he said, as he gestured for me to go in. And sure enough, the hallway looked exactly like I thought it'd would—dark blue walls and white trim, and I had to keep a hand on it as I walked so I wouldn't fall over.

I don't understand, I thought, a wave of dizziness hitting me again so hard I had to stop where I was and close my eyes.

"Reid? Did you get too hot?"

"Hmm?" I managed. I heard Ollie lower the bags to the floor, and then the back of his hand was on my forehead and then my cheek, checking my temperature, and then he took my wrist, checking my pulse.

"The heat index is still over ninety, so you need to cool off," he said, leading me over to a recliner chair and forcing me into it. He returned a few seconds later with a glass of iced water, but my hands were still shaking so badly that he had to lift it to my lips.

It couldn't be heat stroke that had me feeling so strange? No, I didn't think so, but the cold water helped, and when Ollie went back to refill the glass, he also brought a cold towel, placing it around my neck.

"Is that better?" he asked, taking my wrist again and looking at his watch for a full minute. Then he let go and adjusted the towel. "You can lie back if you want to."

I could only stare at him. It was like I was looking at him through new eyes. The way he took such great care with me, completely putting aside any hurt from the night before to make sure I was okay... It was then that I realized how lucky I was that he'd been the one to pull me out of the car.

"I'm sorry, Ollie."

"It's okay. I'm just glad you made it here instead of passing out on the sidewalk."

"No, I mean I'm sorry for last night."

"Oh." He lifted the water back up to my mouth for me to take a sip. "That's okay too."

"I was horrible to you. I feel like I've been horrible to everyone lately, and I was going to call you and tell you...I'm sorry. You didn't deserve my wrath."

Ollie's eyes bored into mine from where he knelt in front of me, and then he nodded. "Thank you. Apology accepted."

The easy way he forgave made my eyes sting, and I had to look down at my lap so he didn't see it. After a moment, he got to his feet and went over to retrieve the bags he'd left in the hallway. I was tempted to go help him, but I didn't think my legs were quite steady enough yet, so I watched as he slid the bags up his arm again and carried them into the adjoining kitchen. It was then that I got a good look of where I was. Sitting up, I took in the straightforward decor: cream-colored walls, oversized grey couches, an entertainment center with a TV that just barely fit inside it. Nothing fancy, but all well maintained, just like the man himself. But what surprised me the most was the piano in the corner of his kitchen.

"You have a piano?" I said, my brows pinching together. "But...you don't play. Do you use it as a table?"

"Hah, very funny, smartass. I think what you mean is I don't play *well*. I do a pretty mean 'Twinkle, Twinkle, Little Star,' though. My teacher may disagree."

"Um. He'd probably say there's room for improvement."

"That would be far too kind of him," Ollie said, chuckling. "So, just out of curiosity, how'd you find me?"

And there was the question I didn't have an answer to. One I wanted to know myself. "I, uh, didn't realize I had."

Ollie continued unpacking the grocery bags and smirked. "Going door to door to ask for me, then? That's stalker behavior, Reid. You could've just called me for my address."

"No, I mean I didn't know this was your house. I don't know why I'm here."

His hands froze as he looked up at me. "I don't understand."

"I don't either." I leaned forward and ran my hands through my hair. "I-I was going for a walk, and I saw your house, and I swore that there was a loose brick on your porch step, and I had to...check. I don't know why, but I had to see if I was right. And your walls?" I gestured down the hallway. "I knew what they looked like before I set a foot inside. Does that make sense to you? Does any of this make sense? Because I feel like I'm fumbling around in the dark, and when I'm awake all I see are these crazy images."

"What kind of images?" Ollie asked, his voice flat and his hands still frozen.

"Don't take this the wrong way, but you. I see you everywhere, but nowhere that makes any sense to me, and I'm just so fucking confused, Ollie." Looking up at him, I gripped the back of my neck and said, "I don't have any explanation for any of this. Not why I'm here, not how I know these things, none of it."

Ollie's Adam's apple bobbed as he swallowed, and his eyes suddenly glistened with tears. "I know you don't," he whispered, his voice shaking as his hands curled into fists. Then he closed his eyes and took a deep, shuddering breath, and when he let it out, he shook his head. "I'm sorry, Reid. I'm so sorry. But I can't do this anymore."

CHAPTER NINE

OLLIE

I DIDN'T KNOW what it was exactly that made me decide to tell Reid the truth. It could've been the desperate plea for help that I heard in his voice, or the way his eyes looked up at me, so full of sadness and doubt. But the time for hiding the truth was over. I'd never wanted to lie to him, but here he was, trying to piece the puzzle of his life back together, and I'd be damned if I didn't give him what he wanted. What he deserved.

Coming back into the living room, I took a seat on the couch closest to where Reid sat in the recliner and rested my arms on my knees. There was a good possibility he'd hate me when I'd finished saying my piece, but for once, I wasn't thinking selfishly. The man I loved was suffering, and if there was something I could do to help him, then I was going to do it. It's what I should've done in the first place.

Not wanting him to think I had anything else to hide once the truth was out, I looked him straight in the eye. "I've gone about this all wrong, Reid. I've confused you even more, and for that, I'm so very sorry. I hope you'll forgive me."

"What are you talking about?"

"I promised your mom I'd help you, be there for you as a friend, but Reid... I can't do that anymore."

"But I told you last night was a mistake, and I wasn't thinking clearly. Why can't you—" His words came to an abrupt stop, and his brow furrowed. "Wait, did you say you promised my mom you'd be friends with me?" When I didn't answer, he said, "Ollie, you know my mom?"

"Yes."

"How?"

"We met in the hospital after your accident."

"You mean after my surgery."

"No. I mean after your accident. While you were in a coma."

"What? How?"

I steepled my hands on my knees and blew out a breath. "Because I'd snuck into your room to see you. To make sure you were okay. I shouldn't have been in there at all, but I just... couldn't help myself. Your family walked in before I could leave, and then..."

"Then what?" Reid asked, his voice shaking.

"Then you woke up."

"Okay," he said, staring down at the coffee table, and I could practically see his mind working to put together what I was telling him, but there was no way he'd be able to manage it. Not without *all* the pieces.

God, can I do this? Tell him the truth and risk losing even the promise of having him in my life at all?

But I didn't have a choice. If I had any love or respect for Reid, then he deserved to have the answers. I only prayed he wouldn't hate me or look at me in disgust once all was said and done.

"So you met her then, but that was months ago. I don't get

why you'd promise her you'd befriend me. Do you normally take on sad charity cases?"

"You're not a sad charity case," I said, my tone coming out a lot firmer than I'd intended. "And there are things you need to understand about the months you don't remember. About the time between your accident and the surgery."

"How would you know anything about those months?"

"Because I was there."

He startled. "What?"

"I was there." I let the information sink in a bit and said, "You spent...a lot of time with me."

Reid was shaking his head as he looked at me in disbelief. "I did?"

"Yes."

"Okay," he said, looking down at his clasped hands, and I could see the wheels turning as he processed what I was telling him. "Okay, so...I've been here before?"

"You have."

"Which is why I knew about the step. About the hallway."

"It is."

"Oh God," he said, and cracked a smile as his eyes welled with tears. "Then I'm not going crazy."

That he'd even doubted himself for a minute racked me with guilt. "No. You're not."

He laughed and wiped his eyes with the sleeve of his t-shirt. "And the tacos? You made them for me? With your own seasoning?"

"Yeah, I did."

"Did I think they were as good as you bragged about last night?"

Shit. "You didn't get a chance to try them."

"Why not? Did you burn 'em?"

I shook my head. "That was the night I took you to the hospital." As Reid's smile fell, I rubbed my jaw. "You were having headaches. Horrible headaches. It turned out to be something more serious than expected."

"Was that the night I had surgery for the bleed?"

"Yes."

"So...you saved my life twice."

I didn't answer, letting his deduction linger in the air as a confirmation. Lost in thought, he traced circles on the arm of the chair, while I had to force my leg to stop bouncing up and down from anxiety.

Reid's fingers stopped moving, and his head shot up. "But...the bowling."

"You remember bowling?" I wondered what exactly had him looking scared shitless when that had been such a good night. In an attempt to lighten things, I said, "You were terrible. I'm assuming you remember the gutter balls."

He swallowed hard. "That's...not..." His chest began to move up and down at a rapid pace.

"Tell me," I said.

"Were we...friends?"

"Yes."

"Just...friends?" His breathing was coming so hard that I thought he might hyperventilate, but when I reached toward him to try to calm him down, he jerked away.

"Reid, just breathe. I'll explain everything, but I need you to calm down. Do you need a bag?"

"No, I don't need a bag," he snapped. "I need the truth. I remember"—his face pinched as he shut his eyes and took a deep breath—"I was jealous. Of a guy in a red shirt."

My heart beat wildly in my chest, as the memory of that night came hurtling back in vivid clarity.

"Why would I be jealous of a guy, Ollie?"

"I didn't know you were jealous then."

"*Then?* What does that mean?"

"It means we became...close."

There was a beat. "Close? Like best friends close?"

I shook my head. "Not just best friends, no." Reid stared at me, and I couldn't tell if he wasn't comprehending, or if he was in shock. "Do you understand what I'm telling you?"

"No," he whispered, but his face betrayed the lie.

"Do you remember anything else? About me? About us?"

"Us," he repeated, clenching his jaw. "No, I can't say I remember any 'us.' Is there something you'd like to fill me in on?"

I could already feel the tide turning, Reid's defensive walls going up even as he listened. The open mindset wasn't there, though, which meant no matter what I said, this was not going to turn out well.

With a sickening sense of dread in my gut, I said, "Let me just say first that I've always had your best interests at heart, Reid. I swear to God. I would never do anything to hurt you or force you to do anything you don't want to do. I never have, and I never will."

"Right. Sure. So can we maybe skip to the part where there's an 'us'? Because I'd really like to hear what the fuck you say I chose to do while I was temporarily out of my head."

Fuck. He was angry. Confused. Alarmed. And so very angry. I'd thought about showing him the note I carried around from him in my pocket, but there was no way I was giving him that sacred piece of the puzzle tonight. Not when he was like this.

"I care about you, Reid. And for a while there...you cared about me too. That's all that matters."

His nostrils flared as he stared at me, his jaw clamped shut so tight that I thought he might break a molar. When he spoke again, it was through clenched teeth. "I don't...believe you."

"Okay." I didn't know what else to say, because there wasn't anything. He could choose to believe me or not, but something told me he already knew the truth and just didn't want to face it. It was a hell of a lot to take in, I knew that, and so I kept my mouth shut even though I wanted to refute his words. I wanted to tell him how much he meant to me, how much our time together had changed my life. I wanted him to remember the days he spent laughing with me and the nights he'd spent in my bed. More than anything, I wanted him to know *us* again. To remember the song he played just for me, and to feel him touch me again just because he wanted to be close. But I was already pushing my luck. I'd never expected to be having this conversation with Reid, and the fact that he'd remembered anything at all about our time together was a gift, even if it didn't feel like one at the moment.

"You're trying to tell me you were my..." He cursed, unable to say the word.

"Boyfriend?" I suggested. "Lover?"

His eyes widened, and he jumped to his feet. "This is insane. *You're* insane. I don't think it's me that's lost my mind here." He stumbled past the coffee table, tripping on the rug in his haste to leave.

"Reid, please don't go. Just stay so we can talk this out—"

"Pretty sure we're done with this conversation."

"Reid—" I followed him down the hallway and caught up with him as he swung open the door. "Wait, please."

He spun around and held his hand out, and if looks could kill, his eyes would've cut me in two. "Get away from me. I don't want you coming any closer. And I don't want you to follow me. I mean it. Just leave me alone."

"You know me, Reid. I'm not the bad guy here. Just let me explain—"

"No," he said, shaking his head. "You're wrong. I don't know you. I don't even know myself anymore. And more than that, I don't think I want to."

Then he backed away before turning and running out of my house—and out of my life. And this time, I had a feeling it was for good.

CHAPTER TEN

REID

THE WIND BLEW *a soft breeze across my skin where I lay on a blanket in the thick grass, my legs stretched out and my head in Ollie's lap. He'd wanted to work on some things around the house, small fixes or painting the shutters or something, but I wasn't letting him get much done today.*

"Truth or dare?" I said, and Ollie's hand stilled where he'd been running his fingers through my hair.

"Really?"

"Yes, really. Truth or dare?"

"I'm a little scared of what you'd make me do if I chose dare, so...truth."

"Truth it is," I said, and chewed on my lip as I thought of a question. "Okay, got it. Have you ever been in love?"

He raised a brow. "That's a loaded question."

"I'm just curious."

"What if you don't like the answer?"

"Ollie..."

"Fine." He sighed and looked out across the yard as his fingers began to move through my hair again. "Once, a long time ago, I thought I was in love."

"You 'thought'? Why do I hear a 'but' in there?"

"I'm pretty sure now that it was simply infatuation. Or maybe love on a smaller scale. Like loving the person, but not being in love with them."

"How do you figure the difference?"

He looked down at me. "Because when someone else comes along and blows away every dream and expectation you ever had, no one else means a damn thing. Past, present, or future."

My heart swelled to bursting as I asked, "Do you think you could love someone like me?"

He smiled and pushed my hair off my forehead. "Yes. I do."

The unspoken words hovered in the air, but I held back from saying them, instead sitting up and pushing Ollie to the ground. He let out a surprised laugh as I straddled his hips.

"There something you want?" he asked, a teasing smile on his lips.

My erection strained against my pants as I leaned over him, grinding myself over the top of him as his cock swelled in response to mine. "Mhmm," I said, as I bit down gently on his full lower lip.

"Tell me," he murmured against my mouth.

"I think you know."

He pulled his head back, and I fell into his warm green gaze. "Tell me anyway."

"I want you, Ollie." I brushed a kiss across his lips and whispered, "I'll always want you."

I woke up with a jolt, panting as I sat straight up in my bed. Sweat trickled down my neck as I brought my fingers to my mouth, the feel of Ollie's lips still velvety soft on mine. My dick jerked under the flimsy material of my briefs, my body responding favorably to the memory. Because that's what it was, wasn't it? A memory. Not a dream. Not a hallucination. A fucking memory.

I'd been with Ollie. I'd *been* with Ollie. *Ollie.* No matter how I tried to say it, I couldn't wrap my brain around what I knew now to be true. All I'd done for the past seventy-two hours was lie here and try to filter through the chunks and fragments I remembered to make sense of things. Well, I'd alternated between the bed and the couch, and at one point I ordered pizza so I wouldn't have to venture out anywhere or starve, but other than that, the only thing that moved was my mind.

My thoughts shuffled between things making sense but not making sense. That I wasn't going crazy was a relief, but it was such a shock to my system that I'd apparently fallen for a man. I hadn't seen that part coming, and my family sure as hell hadn't dropped any hints that they'd known. Had they known? Or had I hidden him away completely? But Ollie said he spoke with my mother, that she'd come to him recently, which led me to believe she knew something. She had to. Had she approved? Had my father? *God, this is too surreal for words,* I thought as I put my head in my hands.

And then there'd been the memories of the time I'd spent with Ollie. They were no longer showing up as just bits of platonic scenes, but as part of something deeper, a relationship that hadn't at all been one-sided. If anything, it was almost as if I'd been the one to pursue *him*, which at first made me wonder how hard I'd hit my head, but the more I thought about it, the more I could almost begin to understand the appeal. After all, in my interactions with him since the day he'd walked into my classroom had proven that he was a caretaker at heart, someone who could be depended on in a crisis or even day to day. He didn't take himself too seriously, as his piano skills and self-deprecating jokes showed, and there was something just *good* about him. Not to mention his arms were something out of *Men's Muscle* magazine. And I guess if you lined up a hundred guys, he'd be the best-looking one out of the bunch, not that I'd ever noticed a guy's looks before. All in all, looking at it objectively—which meant when I wasn't downing a Crown and Coke—he could be considered a catch for anyone. Anyone in the world, and somehow he'd chosen me. Or I'd chosen him.

Ollie...and me. Together. Like...*together* together. *Fuck.*

Oh, and I couldn't forget that he'd lied. Lied by omission, which was still lying. Coming around, getting to know me as if we were strangers, when the whole time he knew exactly how to play me. Showing up at the Music Junction had to have been my mother's idea, because Ollie wouldn't have known about my last-minute fill-in otherwise. Which meant he also knew I didn't drive and would need a ride. *But he knew exactly how to help you when you came across the accident and panicked the hell out.*

"Shut up," I said. "Just shut up."

Ripping off the sheet, I tumbled out of the bed and filled a glass with water. I chugged the entire thing down in one go and then wiped the sweat off my forehead. I had to stop obsessing over this, or I was going to go crazy. If I hadn't already.

An insistent knock sounded at my front door. I hadn't ordered more food, and no one had called at the gate, which meant it could only be one of two people, and I wasn't in the mood for lectures.

I swung open the door and leaned against it as my mom lowered her arm. Even on a Saturday in the middle of summer, she looked the part of a prim school teacher: a pale yellow skirt that fell to her knees and a simple white blouse with pearls. No need for the matching jacket in this heat.

"What are you doing here?" I said.

"You haven't answered my calls or returned messages. I needed to make sure you were alive in here." She lifted an eyebrow as her assessing gaze took in my bare chest and boxer briefs and what I knew had to be disheveled hair, since I hadn't brushed it in three days. "You look awful."

"Thank you. I've been better." I scratched the stubble on my jaw, which wasn't quite as prickly now, given that I hadn't bothered with a razor lately either.

Her smile was hesitant. "May I come in?"

I held the door open, and she walked inside, looking around at the discarded pizza boxes and plates on the counter, and the almost-empty bottle of Crown.

"Good to see you've been staying hydrated," she said wryly as she eyed the liquor and continued on to the living room while I grabbed a shirt and shorts from my room and threw them on. I let her comment pass, not caring one way or another if she knew I'd been self-medicating. She placed her purse on the coffee table and cleared off a space to sit, folding the rumpled blanket neatly before placing it over the back of the couch.

"Make yourself at home," I said, flopping on the other sofa and rubbing my eyes.

"Do you mind telling me what's going on with you, Reid?"

"Actually, I do mind."

"It wasn't a suggestion."

I sat up and crossed my arms over my chest. "Weeell, what isn't going on with me nowadays? Hmm. For starters, I don't remember the last time I played the piano, and I'm really feeling the need to bang on some keys right about now."

"Then why don't you?"

With my eyebrows raised, I looked around the room. "You see one anywhere?"

"No, but—"

"Is there one over at your place I've somehow missed on my visits?"

"Oh. Well, no—"

"That's right," I said, slapping my knee. "Because you and Dad got rid of the piano." God, I sounded like an asshole, but I couldn't stop myself. If I had to be miserable, so did every-fucking-one else. They were all goin' down with me. "Huh. Now why would you do a thing like that?"

Mom blinked at me like I'd lost my mind, and then her small shoulders lifted. "From what I remember, you moved out, and your father wanted room for his desk."

"Ahh. And when you chose this place, did you know about the noise ordinance before or after?"

"What do you mean?"

"My piano, Mom. You know, my passion, my life. The thing I love that I conveniently can't have here?"

"What?" she said. "Do you think we chose this place to keep you from playing?"

"I don't know. Did you?"

"That's ridiculous. How could you think I'd take away something so important to you? Do you really think I'm that malicious?"

"I wouldn't have thought so, no. But I can't help but wonder. I mean, you guys never agreed with my career; you wanted me back here near you and following in your line of work. Maybe you thought I'd forget."

"I wasn't even thinking, Reid. Your father and I thought this would be a nice place for you, gated and with great views. I promise it didn't even cross my mind that you couldn't bring your piano along. And then with you teaching music at the school and having access to several there… I'm so sorry. It honestly didn't cross my mind."

I could only stare at her, the woman who had been my rock for my whole life. The woman who would do anything for anyone and didn't have a mean bone in her body. I knew she hadn't intended to hurt me. I knew it'd been an accident, but I still felt the need to blame someone for all the fuck-ups happening in my life. And truthfully, now that I'd said my piece, I found the anger dissipating like early morning fog, and in its place—the guilt from lashing out. God, I'd been such an ass lately. *What's wrong with me?*

Sighing, I ran a hand over my hair. "I know, Mom. I don't mean to take out my frustration on you."

"Oh, Reid," she said, scooting to the edge of the couch to rub my arm. "I don't pretend to know what's happening to you right now. I know you're confused and upset and taking it out on those closest to you. I know that, and I can handle it. So if you need to vent and yell, I understand. If you want to talk, I'm here. If you have questions, I'll try to help you answer them as best I can. Things *will* get easier, baby. Please believe that."

I wanted to believe she was telling the truth, that she was all-powerful and could see months and years into the future to know it would all turn out okay.

"If you'd like, why don't you get dressed and we can run down to Newton's now and pick out a new piano? The desk has become nothing but a clutter magnet anyway." She squeezed my arm. "I'm so sorry, Reid. I just assumed since Ollie bought one for you to play, that you'd—"

I flinched and pulled away from her. "He did what?"

She seemed to realize her mistake as soon as she said it. "Oh. Oh dear."

"He bought me a piano?"

"Well, I...I didn't realize he had until recently, and—" She stopped and then said a word I hadn't heard come out of her mouth ever: "*Shit.*"

My eyes widened. "Did you just say...'shit'?"

"No," she said, the look on her face a mixture of mortification and embarrassment. "Of course not."

A snort of laughter left me then, because holy fuck—my

proper, kind mother had cursed, which meant hell must've frozen over.

"It's not funny," she said, covering her face when I laughed harder. "Don't tell your father."

"It's just a word, Mom. I don't think it means you've cursed your soul for all eternity." As she continued to shake her head, I rolled the words she'd uttered around in my head. *I just assumed since Ollie bought one for you to play...*

He bought me a *piano*?

"Did you..." I started.

"Yes?"

"Did you know about me and...Ollie?"

She looked me in the eye and said, "We never talked about it, but I knew."

"How?"

"Call it mother's intuition. You spent a lot of time with him after your accident. You told me he was someone who felt familiar to you, and...I noticed you smiled a lot more when he was in the picture."

I swore my heart skipped a few beats as I listened to what she was telling me. She knew. She'd *known*. And somehow, she wasn't judging me at all. My world tilted on its axis.

"Did Dad know?" I asked.

"It doesn't matter—"

"Did Dad know, Mom?"

"No. No, I never said anything."

"Why?"

"Because it wasn't important," she said firmly. "You were happy. That's all that ever matters. That you're safe and you're happy."

"But—"

"No buts, Reid. Why do you think I went to Ollie to help you? It was because I've never seen you happier in your entire life than you were in those few weeks. I didn't need confirmation or details to know what had changed."

My mouth opened and shut a few times as I processed what she was saying. I'd been happy? Not only happy, but happier than I'd ever been in my *life*? With Ollie? I thought about the memory from this morning, how the words *I love you* had been on the tip of my tongue, the feeling so strong that it almost overwhelmed me. And the memory I'd awoken to yesterday, when he'd taken me to a place that looked like something out of *The Wizard of Oz*, and I'd had a strong feeling of an entirely different sort.

"You're saying you were okay with me being...being..." I gripped the back of my neck and looked up at the ceiling, as if that would have the answers I was looking for.

"With a man?" Mom said, and my eyes met hers again. There was such love and acceptance in her gaze, and it made my heart constrict. "But Ollie's not just any man, is he?"

I swallowed past the lump in my throat.

"He never left that waiting room after your surgery. Even when you woke up and had no idea who he was. He waited, and I don't think he ever gave up hope that you'd find your way back to him. Then you came home, and he called every single day to check on you. For over a month, like clockwork, until the doctor told us it was likely you may never remember the weeks you lost. At the time, I thought maybe it was best to focus on what was familiar to you. Surround you with the people you knew and loved before your accident." She shook her head. "But I was wrong to make him stay away. I take full responsibility for my actions, and I've apologized to Ollie too."

My breaths came out shallow as I rested my head in my hands, trying to combine the worlds that warred in my brain. "I don't understand how this happened."

"Sometimes life takes unexpected turns and gives you a good

wallop on the head to make you see things clearly—Oh, I didn't mean your accident, good grief. That was a bad choice of words."

I chuckled softly. "No offense taken."

"How do *you* feel? Things are coming back to you now?"

"Mom, I... I don't know how to feel." I twisted my fingers together as I searched for what to say. "I thought I was going crazy. I thought I was having hallucinations, honest to God. I had no idea I was remembering things that really happened. And now that I know?" I shook my head. "I'm even more lost than I was before."

"Oh, baby," she said, and moved over to the couch beside me, holding me close as I held on to her like a life preserver. "I wish I could help you make sense of things. I wish I could make it easy."

"I can't decide if it's a good or bad thing to remember," I said, my voice muffled in her shirt.

"It doesn't have to be one or the other. This isn't something you have to rush to understand overnight. You have all the time in the world to figure out how you want to live your life and who the people are that you want in it."

"Do I?" I asked, straightening. "Have all the time in the world now?" I found that hard to believe after everything I'd gone through this year.

"Yes. I believe you really do. I think you've been given a fresh start. But don't keep carrying around all this heavy weight and guilt. Don't drown your mind in alcohol and shut yourself away in here. That's not you, and that's never been you."

My gaze drifted over to the littered countertop. "I know. You're right."

"And hey? If you want a piano, we'll get one. If you decide teaching isn't for you and you want to try something else, then do it. I won't try to know what's best for you anymore, Reid, because I'm getting it wrong at every turn. Only you can figure out what you need to make you happy."

I hadn't realized how much I needed to hear those words from her, but they soothed some of the ache in my soul that had been taking a beating since I'd moved back to Floyd Hills, a failure with my tail between my legs. I wasn't the same man I'd been then, only a year ago—but the problem was that I had no idea who the hell I was now. Staying in my apartment for three days hadn't given me any answers, and it never would.

"Mom, I...I don't know what I'm supposed to do now," I admitted. "About Ollie."

She brushed my hair off my forehead in a tender gesture. "I know you're confused. I know this doesn't make sense to you. And I know that Ollie expects nothing from you. He's not that kind of person. Whether you can find the connection the two of you once shared is entirely up to you, but no matter what, I know that man will be there for you regardless of what you decide. He could be the best friend you'll ever have." When she blinked, a tear fell down her cheek, and she smiled at me and cupped my face. "And I think you need that, Reid. I really do."

CHAPTER ELEVEN

OLLIE

REID WASN'T AT the Music Junction on Sunday for the piano class. I'd debated whether to go at all, but after deliberating for all of five seconds, I'd decided I wasn't letting him or anyone else scare me away this time. He'd told me before his surgery to fight for him, for us, and that was what I planned to do. I'd be there for him, through all of the confusion, all of his anger. Because the fact was that Reid remembered me. Not everything, not nearly everything, but he knew who I was to him now. Or who'd I'd been. And though our fate rested solely in his hands, I would do everything in my power to tip the scales and give us another chance.

But as I lifted the edge of the paper on the classroom door that indicated the lesson had been canceled for the day due to sickness, I sighed. Reid sure wasn't making this easy, was he?

As I got back in my car, I weighed my options. I could go by his place to check on him, see if he really was sick or avoiding me. I could drive over to his parents' place. Or I could call him and see if he needed any chicken soup.

Going with option number three, I scrolled down to Reid's

number and pressed the call button, and then I pulled out of the parking lot. A few seconds later, his voicemail picked up, and I hit *end* instead of leaving a message. I hadn't actually expected him to answer, not after the way he'd left my place a few days ago. I was hoping giving him time to cool off and deal with what he'd learned was the smart thing to do, but I had no idea how to play this. I wasn't ready to lose Reid again, not now, not ever, but I didn't want to come on too strong and scare him off either.

I'll wait, I decided, heading toward my house instead of stopping by unannounced at either of his probable destinations. Maybe I'd check in with his mom later, feel her out on his mindset and go from there.

Jesus, it's hot, I thought, flipping the air up as the afternoon sun fried me from all sides. In my attempt to look nice for Reid, I'd worn a dress shirt with a pair of pressed slacks, but now the clothes felt stiffing, and I unbuttoned the collar, finally able to breathe. I was more than ready to get into some worn jeans and a damn t-shirt. As I pulled into my neighborhood, "Love Bites" by Def Leppard came on, and I turned the volume up to deafening as I sang along. God, the chorus was accurate right about now. Love did fucking bleed and bring you to your knees, didn't it? I was in the middle of belting a high note as I reached my house when my voice faltered at the sight in front of me.

Reid was sitting on my porch.

My mouth clamped shut as I switched off the radio. *Well I'll be damned.*

When he saw me pull in, he stood up, dusting his shorts off. I didn't think I'd ever seen him so casual, but a white tank top, shorts, and flip-flops definitely worked for him. Fuckin' hell, he was gorgeous, no matter what he wore. Or didn't wear. *Don't think about that, for fuck's sake.* I kept my sunglasses on as I got out of the car, not wanting him to read too much into whatever look I threw his way, because I wasn't sure what he'd see. Longing? Desire? Hurt? A combination of the three?

"Hi," I said when I walked up, keeping things light as I came to a stop in front of him and assessed his mood. "Missed you at class today. You contagious?"

"Am I what?"

"The note on the door said you were sick."

"Oh. I lied. I'm taking a mental health day." Inclining his head toward the door, he said, "Can we talk?"

"Sure."

He followed me inside, and I willed my hands not to shake, but fuck I was nervous. I didn't know if it was a good thing he was here or not, or whether this visit would lead to somewhere good or somewhere I'd rather not think about. As we entered the living room, I tossed my keys on the entertainment center, and when I turned around, Reid regarded my outflt.

"You look"—he seemed to struggle for the word—"nice."

"Thank you," I said, surprised, but trying not to read too much into the fact that he'd noticed what I was wearing or that he thought I looked "nice." "Actually, it's a little warm, so I was gonna change into something a little more comfortable. Can you gimme a sec?"

"Okay." He stood in the middle of the living room, not making a move to sit down, so I gestured around.

"Make yourself at home. Wherever."

I changed quickly, and when I came back out, the door leading out onto the screened-in porch in the backyard was open, and I flled a couple of glasses with iced water before heading out to join Reid there. Without the sun shining down and with the fans going, it wasn't too bad, and I was glad he'd decided to come out here. It felt too claustrophobic inside.

"Thanks," he said, taking the glass I offered.

I settled into one of the Adirondack chairs across from him, set my glass on the table beside me, and waited for him to make the first move.

"Thanks for not slamming the door in my face. I wouldn't have blamed you if you had."

"Slamming doors isn't really my style."

"No, of course not." He shifted in his seat, crossing his ankles and then uncrossing them. "Ollie, I want to apologize for my behavior the other day. To say I was shocked might be the understatement of the year, and I reacted badly. I know I probably said some things that hurt you, and for that I'm so sorry." He twisted his fingers in his lap. "I've been an asshole. Not just to you, but to everyone. I don't want to be that way anymore."

"I'd say that's the first step to recovery."

A hint of a smile lifted his lips. "I'm not going to run or freak out. Well...I may still freak out, I don't know. But I want to understand."

I could read between those lines: he wanted to understand me. Maybe even us. If he couldn't hear the way my heart pounded, I would've been shocked.

"Okay," I managed to say. "I accept your apology."

His shoulders sagged in relief. "Good. That's good."

We fell into silence, with only the whir of the fans and the distant yells and laughing of neighborhood children playing to fill the space between us. I knew there was more weighing on his mind, but I was content to sit there with him for as long as he needed.

Eventually, he said, "Can I ask you a question?"

"You can ask me lots of questions."

"I gravitated toward you because you were familiar to me. That's what my mom said."

"You told me the same."

"I did?"

I nodded.

"But"—his forehead wrinkled—"I'm not sure I follow. How can someone I never met be familiar?"

"Well, we saw each other at Joe's."

"That's it? You were familiar because I passed you getting coffee every morning?"

"That and, you know, pulling you out of a wrecked car. You were coherent enough after your accident that you remembered me."

Reid reared back in his chair. "Oh. I see." He drummed his fingers along the edge of the armrest. "Did I ever thank you for that? For saving me that day?"

I smiled. "You have. Many times."

"Right. Good. At least I never forgot my manners, huh?" he joked. I decided to go along with it, ease the nerves I could see manifesting in his movements.

"Yes, you were always very polite, even when you invited yourself along when I'd go for a run."

His eyes went round. "No, I did not."

"You did," I said, chuckling.

"Oh my God." He groaned and covered his face. "I'm so embarrassed."

"Don't be. I wanted you around. Trust me."

"But that sounds like pest behavior. Are you sure you weren't just feeling sorry for me?"

"Definitely not," I said, as he lifted his head. "I was flattered by your attention. I wanted more of it."

Reid took a deep breath and bit down on his bottom lip, and I wondered if I'd gone too far. Was I supposed to remind him of my affection for him? Keep it friendly? There wasn't a guidebook to steer me in the right direction of "how not to scare off your brain-injured exes," so I was winging it the best I could.

"I've been thinking," he said slowly. "I'd like to get to know you, Ollie. Again. If you'll let me."

I had to look down as the sting behind my eyes made it clear tears were well on their way, and I thought for a minute I'd need a defibrillator to jolt my heart back into beating. I never thought I'd hear those words from him. I never thought he'd be sitting across from me, ready and willing to open himself up again, and even though he still seemed hesitant and a bit shy, the fact that he was here meant everything.

"Ollie, I can't...promise anything—"

"Stop," I said, holding up my hand. "Just stop. I don't expect anything from you, Reid. I'm not here to force you into spending time with me if that's not what you want."

"Is that what *you* want?"

I stared at him incredulously. "Of course it is."

"Okay. Well, I certainly know that the dreams I've been having about us mean you don't want to talk me out of it, so how about we just go with it for now?" he said, and my mouth fell open at his matter-of-fact tone. "Oh, and another thing—I'd like you to take me out driving."

My jaw dropped even farther.

"I don't want to be afraid anymore, and what better person to be there if I have a panic attack than you, right?"

I was speechless. Utterly fucking speechless.

"So if it's all right with you, maybe you can help me one night this week after work," he said. It must've occurred to him then that I hadn't agreed yet, because he frowned. "Have I shocked you mute? Nod once if you understand."

I nodded once.

"Okay, nod twice if you'll take me driving and play whatever song you were jamming out to when you pulled in today."

Oh shit. I'd been busted. I nodded twice.

A smile crossed Reid's face then, the first one I'd seen since he sat down, and it reminded me so much of the way he'd smiled at me before that it was like a physical tug on my heart. He scooted to the edge of his seat and held his hand out to shake mine. His long fingers were cool from where they'd been wrapped around the glass, a welcome relief from my always-scorching palms.

"Well, Ollie," he said. "It looks like we have a deal."

CHAPTER TWELVE

REID

IT HAD BEEN a restless night, and an even more restless day. Ever since I'd left Ollie's house after our talk the evening before, I'd been barraged with memories of him, like my mind was having a picture show with no intermission in sight. It was as if when I'd finally given myself permission to understand and explore a possible friendship with Ollie, my brain let loose, like water bursting through a dam after a long shutdown. And with the memories came the feelings I'd associated with them as they'd happened, and that was the part I was desperately trying to work through. All the feelings of longing, of lust, and even the other L-word I couldn't begin to bring myself to think about. It all hit me full force while lying in bed, while in the shower, while making lunch. I'd given up trying to drown it out with TV, because what did you need a television for when your mind was a twenty-four-seven Netflix binge?

It was nuts. Fucking nuts. And it wouldn't go away.

After a long, hot shower, I threw on the first shirt I saw in my closet, but after glancing in the mirror, I ripped it off and tried another. And then another. Tonight Ollie would be picking me up after he got off work, which meant I'd had a long day to stress about seeing him again, and I didn't want to look too dressed up, like I was trying too hard. Shorts would be too casual, so those were out...maybe jeans? Ten shirts later, I finally settled on a deep ruby one and then stepped into the bathroom to shave. But as I lifted the razor, my mind drifted.

"I like this," Ollie said, running his thumb along the edge of my five o'clock shadow.

"Do you?" I'd meant to shave that morning, but I'd been in a rush to see him and it slipped my mind. "So I should keep it?"

"You look hot as fuck either way. But this"—he leaned in and brushed his stubbled cheek against mine—"would feel damn good against my thighs..."

Holy fuck. My heart thudded at the memory...and I put the razor down.

True to his word, Ollie was waiting in the parking lot of my apartment complex at six p.m. on the dot, and as I walked out of my place and caught sight of him below, the apprehension I'd been feeling all day about seeing him again disappeared.

He was leaned against the hood of his car, his massive arms crossed over his broad chest, the black t-shirt he wore stretched to its limits. His hair looked darker, but as I came down the stairs and got a better view, I realized that was because it was wet, like he'd come straight over after a shower. The effect was...well, unnerving, if the way my stomach flipped was any indication.

"Hey there," he said, pushing off the hood and giving me a crooked grin. I wasn't sure whether I should give him a hug or shake his hand or fist-bump or whatever it was we were supposed to do to greet each other, so I came to a stop in front of him and waited to see what he'd do. Like he sensed my uncertainty, he shoved his hands in his pockets, giving me an out I wasn't sure I wanted.

"Hey. Just get off work?" I asked. *Duh, of course he did. You already knew that.*

"Yeah," he said, ducking his head and running his hand through the damp strands like he was self-conscious he hadn't had a chance to dry them. I wanted to tell him he didn't need to be, because wet was a good look for him, but maybe that wasn't the best way to start off the conversation.

"So...how was your day?" I asked.

"It was a little rough. Much better now."

"I'm sorry to hear that," I said, and then shook my head. "I mean the rough part, not the better now part."

He chuckled and rocked back on his heels. "I know what you meant."

What the hell is wrong with me? My stomach felt like a hundred goddamn butterflies had been unleashed since I'd come down the stairs. It was just Ollie, for God's sake. There wasn't any reason to be nervous. He was the same guy I'd seen yesterday, the same one I'd had dinner and drinks with last week with Mike and Deb. But somehow he looked different to me, and I couldn't put my finger on why.

"I thought we'd take it slow tonight. Start you off on back roads and see how you go," he said, breaking the silence.

"Yeah, back roads are great. Good plan."

"Cool. So"—he held up a set of keys—"you wanna do the honors?"

I stared at the keys for a second. "Ohh. You meant you want me to start us out from here. My bad." *Hello, a little slow on the uptake there, Reid.*

"Unless you'd prefer I take us out first and then switch?"

"Nope, I got this," I said, feigning confidence. I'd been so preoccupied with thoughts of Ollie all night and day that it had barely even occurred to me that I'd be driving for the first time since my accident all those months ago. That only made my nerves ratchet up a few hundred notches. No big deal. "Hand 'em on over."

He placed the keys in my open palm, and as his skin grazed mine...there it was. That spark that shocked me when we touched, and this time, I could see he felt it too, because he jerked at the same time. I gulped and pulled my hand away.

"I guess we should..." I gestured to the car, and he nodded.

"Yeah, we should."

As I climbed into the driver's seat, I wondered if I'd ever been so on edge in my life, and it had everything to do with the man sliding in beside me. I tried not to focus on how close we were in such a small space, but that was easier said than done with the smell of his heady cologne filling my nose. I'd smelled it on him before, but never thought twice about it, and now all I could think about was what kind it was and where exactly he'd sprayed it.

Focus, Reid. Jesus.

I buckled myself in and adjusted the mirrors, and then I sat with my hands at ten and two, giving myself a quick *don't freak the fuck out* talk.

"You ready for this?" Ollie asked, and I leaned back against the headrest and looked at him. His eyes were so intense, seeing right through my anxiety, and the compassion I found in their depths helped set my mind at ease.

My stuttering heart, however, was a different story.

"Um." I shifted in my seat. "Is it weird that I'm nervous?" *And not just about the driving.*

"Not at all. Take your time. There's no rush."

I blew out a breath and wiped my hands on my pants. Then I adjusted the mirrors again, made sure my seat was comfortably positioned—basically, I was procrastinating. Out of the corner of my eye, Ollie took his sunglasses off from where they'd been hanging on his shirt, but as he unfolded them, I blurted out, "Don't put those on."

His hand halted. "Why not?"

"Because then I can't see your eyes."

Ollie stared at me for a long moment, and without a word, he folded the glasses and put them in the glove compartment.

"Okay," I said, cranking the car. "Here we go."

I took it slow through the parking lot, getting used to the feel of the vehicle, tapping the brakes to see how much give they had. As we came out of the gated complex, I stopped before the main road.

"Let's make a left here, and then we'll go up Harris and make a wide loop," he said.

"Sounds good to me." I flipped on the blinker and waited for several cars to pass before I made the turn. Ollie sat patiently next to me, letting me take my time instead of pointing out all the missed opportunities to pull out. In that respect, he was the perfect person to take me back on the road, and I was grateful in that moment that I hadn't been a stubborn asshole and stayed cooped up in my apartment.

Thanks, Mom...

The five o'clock traffic had simmered down, and the way we were going meant there wouldn't be many other cars around anyway. Sitting behind the wheel again didn't feel as strange as I thought it would, and I was surprised to find that having Ollie with me took my mind off focusing on the what-ifs—trucks T-boning me, basically.

It was so quiet, never a good thing when I had my crazy thoughts to occupy me, so I said, "Did you want to turn on the radio?"

"Nah, we probably don't need the distraction."

Yeah, you're enough of a distraction. "Damn. I was so hoping to get a glimpse of karaoke Ollie."

"Oh God." He laughed. "Unless I'm alone in the car, it'll take me about ten margaritas before you catch an earful of me singing."

"Say it ain't so."

"It's so all right. It's not just the words I butcher. I think I'm as bad at singing as I am at the piano."

"Yikes," I said, pretending to cringe. "That's a little scary."

"Hey, isn't that against some kind of teacher handbook to tell a student they suck?"

"I never said you sucked. I said you were scary."

Ollie bristled and shook his head. "I blame the teacher, then. After one class, I should be a goddamn prodigy. I want my money back."

With a laugh, I flipped down the visor to block the sun from blinding me and wondered at how surprised I was by how easy it was to just be with him. I didn't feel any pressure or tension coming from his direction—instead, I simply enjoyed his company. But I wanted to know more. I wanted to know about the day-to-day, and I wanted him to know he could talk to me if he needed to. That was part of this whole *getting to know you again* thing, wasn't it?

"Why was it a rough day at work?" I asked.

"Nah, you don't wanna hear about that."

"I wouldn't have asked if I didn't."

He bit down on his lip for a moment and then nodded. "Sometimes it's just a hard job. No two days are ever the same, which I like, but you never know what you're walking into when you get a call." He looked out the passenger window. "Not everyone has a happy ending."

My heart lurched at the sadness in his tone. "I don't know how you do it. How you don't carry all that home with you."

"Oh, but I do," he said. "Most of the people I work with, they've got kids or partners to come home to. I don't really have any diversions to keep my mind from replaying what I call the *could've-should'ves*. I think a lot about the patients that come through, about how they're faring or what I could've done differently. It weighs on me a bit." He gave me a tight smile. "And now I bet you're thinking that's too heavy of an answer."

"No. I was thinking it takes a special person to be able to handle a job like yours."

His smile grew a little bigger. "I appreciate you saying that."

"It's the truth. I could never do a job where people's lives were in my hands."

"You'd be surprised what you find you can do that you never imagined. I mean, look at you and all you've been through. It hasn't been easy, but you're trying. Right? And I bet it would've seemed impossible before. Thriving and driving," he said, chuckling.

Thriving and driving was right. It hadn't been nearly as scary as I thought it would be. The drive had been a smooth one, exactly like riding a bike for the first time after a long winter. I wasn't as rusty as I thought, and that had me feeling brave.

"Ollie? I think...I'd like to go back," I said.

"No problem. I can take you back if you want. Just pull over when it's clear," he said, reaching down to unbuckle his seatbelt.

"No, I mean...back to where it happened."

"Oh," Ollie said, his eyebrows lifted. "Are you sure?"

"I'd rather face it for the first time with you than on my own." I glanced at him. "Is that okay?"

"It's more than okay," he said. His vote of confidence made me smile, and I turned us around in the direction of downtown.

But the closer we got to where it'd all gone done, the more my self-assurance faded. By the time I turned onto Mercer, my hands were full-on trembling.

"You're doing great, Reid," he said, his encouragement exactly the thing I needed to hear as we traveled down Mercer, coming up to the intersection at Thomas, where I'd been blindsided by a truck that January morning.

The light was red as we approached the intersection, and I slowed to a stop, my hands clenched tightly around the wheel. Neither of us spoke as we sat there, waiting for the light to change. When it turned green, I stayed where I was for another few seconds, looking on all sides for anyone who'd decided to disregard their red light. Then I cautiously crossed over Thomas, right over where my car had been hit, and as soon as I passed it, I let out the breath I'd been holding.

"You did it," Ollie said, grinning at me, and I couldn't help but smile back. It may have seemed like such a small step to anyone else, but to me, I'd just faced one of my fears head-on, and the relief I felt was enormous. I figured I would have to work my way up to driving down here, but I'd done it. I'd actually freaking done it. And even though it would still probably be a while before I was comfortable driving again, at least I didn't have to be afraid of having a panic attack on the road anymore.

"Fuck," I said, my heart still pounding as I pulled the car into a bank parking lot and put it in park.

"You okay?"

"Yeah, I am. That was kind of a rush." I reached for the air conditioning dial at the same time Ollie did, and when his arm brushed against mine, goosebumps skated across my skin. But this time I didn't flinch. He noticed.

After turning the AC up a bit higher, he leaned back in his seat, turning slightly to face me. And then, like he was testing out the waters, he said, "I like the red on you."

Looked like my time spent getting ready hadn't been a waste, after all, especially when Ollie's gaze settled on the line of my jaw. Without him even touching me, I shivered, wondering if the memory that had made me put my razor away was the same one that had his tongue running along his lower lip now.

"I don't know what you have planned," he said, his eyes flicking up to mine, "but I'm having to use some of my vacation time this week before it expires, so let me know if you want to do this again."

The time he'd taken me up to one of his favorite spots crossed my mind, and it gave me an idea. "Does that mean you're free all day tomorrow?"

"If you want me to be."

"I want you to be."

"Then I'm all yours."

"Good." My cheeks heated under his potent stare. I was blushing. The man had reduced me to blushing.

When Ollie spoke again, his voice was deep and full of gravel. "Do you want to keep going?" he asked, and it didn't take a genius to know he wanted me to read between the lines: *Do you want to keep going with me?*

"Yes," I said. "I definitely do."

CHAPTER THIRTEEN

OLLIE

"SHOULD I BE worried about where you're taking me?" I said the next morning, as I pushed a wayward branch out of my way and continued up the secluded dirt path leading up an unmarked hill an hour northwest of Floyd Hills.

"Definitely. I think that head bump turned me into a serial killer." Reid looked over his shoulder at me and grinned, and I quickly forced my eyes away from where I'd been staring at his ass. If he didn't want me to look, he wouldn't make me follow him, that was my way of thinking. Hiking up a secluded trail was giving me a prime view, especially with the shorts he wore showing off his leanly muscled legs. It was impossible for me not to think about those legs wrapped around me, which was making my shorts tighten around my hips—not exactly comfortable for a hike.

Stop thinking about him naked, I reminded my dick. *This is a friendly day out, that's all.* Even if the tension in the car on the way up hadn't exactly been what I would call *friendly*. Not with the looks Reid had been throwing my way when he thought I wasn't looking.

"We're almost there," he said, then stopped and held his finger to his lips. "Listen." Without our footsteps crunching over fallen twigs, I could hear the sound of rushing water.

"A waterfall?" I asked. "Is that where we're going?"

Reid zipped his lips and started walking again. The sound grew louder as we traipsed along, and a few minutes later, we were rewarded with one hell of a gorgeous view.

"Wow." That was all I could manage as I gazed up at the towering falls that looked like water pouring out of the sky. Lush green trees and plants surrounded the rocky face, and at its base, mist rose to give the place an ethereal look. It was breathtaking.

"You like things off the beaten path, so I thought you might want to see this. I mean, if you haven't already." Reid chewed on his lip. "It doesn't have a yellow brick road, but..."

Holy shit. He remembers our trip up to the Hidden Land of Oz? "This is incredible," I said, tearing my eyes away from the falls, because even as beautiful as it was, it had nothing on Reid. "I can't believe you remembered."

"I'm starting to remember lots of things," he said, holding my gaze, which made me wonder if those other *things* involved what happened at the end of that date.

As that thought entered my mind, I almost forgot how to breathe until he gave me a small smile and inclined his head. "Come on," he said, walking out onto the rocks that surrounded the pool of water at the base of the waterfall, and I followed.

"We're not, uh, gonna be diving from up there, are we?"

"Definitely not," he said. "The water's not very deep, maybe five feet or so. One head injury is enough for me."

Thank you, Lord. "What a shame. I wasn't nervous about jumping or anything."

"Of course not. Superman's not afraid of much, right?"

What did he just say? Did he call me Superman?

I swallowed. "Right."

Reid took off his backpack and took out an oversized towel, big enough for at least two or three people, and spread it out along a flat surface. Then he gestured around us. "Welcome to Valentine Falls."

"Is that really the name of it?"

"Nah. This is where my mom and dad would bring us on weekends in the summer sometimes. No one ever comes up here, so we thought it was a cool little hidden spot just for us."

Reid peeled off his shoes and socks, and then lifted his shirt up over his head, letting it fall down on top of the backpack. His lean body was creamy perfection, not a blemish or marking anywhere, and I could still feel the way his taut abs felt beneath my fingertips. I didn't try to hide the way I watched him undress —that had always been my favorite part. Watching him slowly reveal himself or letting me do the honors. It didn't escape my notice that after the compliment I'd given him about his red shirt yesterday that he'd chosen to wear a pair of red swim trunks. It made me want to pay him another compliment now, but held my tongue as I toed off my shoes and socks and then stripped out of my shirt.

Reid's eyes trailed down my body, and I stood there unmoving, letting him look at me. It was almost shy the way he looked at me, like he wasn't sure he should but couldn't help himself. I wondered if he remembered me this way, remembered the way my body felt to him, and if it made him want to touch me again.

He backed into the water. "You coming in?"

"I'd love to, but I wish you had told me to bring swim trunks."

Reid stopped moving, and his forehead wrinkled. "I did. Didn't I? Shit." Then he visibly flushed. "You don't really need them, I suppose..."

Smirking, I enjoyed the way he tried to avert his eyes as I reached for the button of my shorts, but I caught him peeking as I lowered the zipper and then let the material fall to my feet.

Reid shook his head, a mixture of disappointment and relief on his face when my swim shorts came into view.

"That's not right and you know it," he said.

"I can take them off if you'd prefer?"

"No, don't do that." He quickly turned away to wade deeper into the water, but not fast enough that I didn't see the way his shorts bulged in the front.

Damn. The thought of me naked had turned him on. And that had me feeling empowered, to know that the attraction Reid had held for me seemed to be making a reappearance. It was almost enough to have me kicking the swim trunks off too, but that might be pushing it for a first date. Wait, was it a date? It sure as hell felt like one to me.

I dipped my toe into the water, and was surprised to find it wasn't freezing cold.

"I thought the water would be unbearable," I said, stepping into the shallow depths. "This isn't too bad, especially in this heat."

Reid swam out past his hips before turning around. "Now you see why we came up here."

"Mhmm. I'm surprised you wanted to share this place with an outsider."

"Well, you're not exactly a stranger, are you? And I knew you'd appreciate somewhere a bit hidden. Not so run over with tourists trying to take selfies and not actually seeing the beauty here at all."

"You've got me pegged, all right," I said, wincing as the water hit the edge of my shorts. "Okay, now it's cold."

"It's less painful if you dive under and get it over with."

"I don't see you in such a hurry to go under."

I barely got the words out before Reid ducked below the surface and emerged a few seconds later. Water dripped off him, his skin deliciously wet and glistening, and as he ran his hand through his hair, he grinned at me. "Your turn."

Not one to back away from a challenge, I dove underwater, swam over to where he was standing, and knocked him off his feet. He was sputtering out a laugh when I stood up, and then he slapped the surface, sending a spray toward my face. Before I could retaliate, he swam out toward the waterfall, and I trailed after him.

It was too loud to hear each other under the falls, so I closed my eyes and let the water beat down over me, washing away all the months of heartbreak and sadness, of anxiety and fear. All the things that had tortured me in my waking hours and again while I slept. The nightmare of Reid forgetting who I was, the reality that I would never be a part of his life when he woke up...I let all that suffering pour out of me. I didn't need to be afraid anymore—my gut told me that. The minute Reid had come over to apologize and open himself up to understanding us was the minute I knew all hope wasn't lost. And the more time we spent together, the more I could see the change in him. The way he looked at me had gone from disoriented to curiosity to interest. His body responded to mine even in the smallest ways, the briefest of touches; the electric current that had always run through us had come back stronger than before. But this time, I didn't have any expectations. I was simply happy to just be with him. Just *be*.

When I opened my eyes, Reid was watching me through the curtain of water, and my dick instantly reacted. I stepped out of the falls and pushed my hair back off my face to see his eyes dilate, and was that...hunger?

"You're"—he slowly shook his head—"really something else. I'm not sure what the right word is."

There was no way he couldn't hear the way my heart faltered for a few beats, but I tried to brush off what he was trying to tell me, because otherwise, I wasn't sure I could keep my hands away from him. "Persistent? Ginger? Bonkers?"

"Beautiful," he said, the word coming out shaky, but without an ounce of sarcasm or a trace of humor. He stood utterly still, memorizing every line of my face, my chest, my arms, and the craziest thing in that moment was that I believed him. The most striking man I'd ever seen thought *I* was beautiful. He kept blowing me away at every turn.

"Reid, you can't keep looking at me that way."

His lips tipped up. "How am I looking at you?"

I let out a groan and swam back a bit. "Like you don't want to take things slow."

"So I can't look at you now, huh? Does that mean it's time for truth or dare instead, then? That's going slow, right?"

I snorted. "Not if our past history is anything to go by, it's not."

Reid dragged his lip between his teeth. "Hmm. You're right about that."

Ahh, so he remembered our past conversation and the *after* that came with it. That meant truth or dare was too dangerous a game to play until he knew for certain that something *more* was what he wanted.

"Well, if you're in the mood to confess, there *is* something I've been wondering about," I said.

"You already know what I look like naked."

With a groan, I plunged back under the water, and when I came back up, I said, "You are not making this easy on me."

Reid smiled, that knowing smile that said he knew what effect he had on me, and if he'd only come a bit closer, he would feel the evidence of my arousal. I needed to veer to another subject and fast.

"The first time I ever saw you, it was at Joe's and you wore this pin on your suit jacket. Like right here on the lapel," I said, running my fingers over the spot. "I never saw you wear it again, and I always wondered if it meant something to you."

"Damn. You really did notice me, huh?"

I rolled my eyes, but knew I sported a cheesy grin on my face. "Well, you don't see many guys wearing one."

"No, I guess you don't," he agreed as he dropped lower so that his shoulders were covered. "It belonged to my grandmother. She was obsessed with birds. She had about fifty birdhouses in her backyard, which was huge, at least a couple of acres. Every day she'd go out there and make sure the feeders were full and dry, and then she'd sit on her back porch and point out what kind they were to whoever was with her that day." His lips quirked up as a faraway look entered his eyes. "Her favorite was the cardinal. She always said those birds were your passed loved ones coming to visit, so all the paintings inside featured them, and she swore my grandfather came to sit on her porch railing every day. He'd given her so much jewelry over the years, but her favorite thing to wear was the silver pair of cardinal wings he'd had engraved with their wedding date. She gave it to me before she passed, and I always wear it for shows or for good luck. I'm guessing if you saw me wearing it, then it was my first day teaching."

"Yeah, you would've needed luck for that. Damn kids," I said, chuckling as a shiver racked my body.

"Cold?"

"Isn't it supposed to warm up the more you swim?"

"Not this one. I think there's a fifteen-minute max. Kinda like a reverse hot tub."

After we got out of the water, we stretched out on the towel, side by side, soaking in the vitamin D as the sun dried us off. Even with room to spare around us, Reid had scooted in close enough that our arms barely touched, and somehow, it was enough. Completely content, I felt myself drifting off into sleep slowly, as I thought about the man beside me. It was an absolutely perfect day. Not a cloud in the sky. No one else around. Nothing could've been better—

"Ollie?"

"Hmm?"

"Am I still your Bluebird?"

—except for that. My eyes opened, spots dotting my vision as I pushed up onto my elbow. Reid stared up at me, his hand shielding the rays, and I found that I was...speechless.

His lips quirked at my stunned expression. "Nothing to say?"

I could only blink at him, and he chuckled. "I always liked that nickname. When I remembered the night at the bowling alley, I didn't understand what it meant, but then I heard your voice telling me to hold on, telling me how you came up with it. I couldn't see you, but I heard you."

Without thinking, I put my hand on the side of his neck and ran my thumb over his lower lip. "You will always be my Bluebird." I felt his chest hitch as I leaned in and pressed a kiss against his forehead. "Thank you for bringing me here."

Fully dried off now, and with the sexual tension creeping back up, I knew if I lay there anymore, I was liable to take this much further than it needed to go, and he wasn't ready for that.

"I think I'm gonna go cool off," I said, getting to my feet, and I didn't bother trying to hide the hard-on I knew was on prominent display. He knew how I felt about him, just as he knew I would never push him to do anything he wasn't ready for.

The water felt even colder after having sunned for a few minutes, but I hadn't gotten past my shins when I heard Reid behind me.

"Ollie?"

I turned around to see him standing at the edge of the towel. "Yeah?"

He took a few steps forward, his stride purposeful and his

hands coming up like he was going to reach out for me, but at the last second, he hesitated and dropped his arms by his sides.

There were one of two things I could do. One, I could pretend I hadn't noticed what he'd been about to do, or two, I could say fuck it and go for it. After all, Reid wasn't looking at me with indecision. No, he was looking at me like he was dying to make the first move but couldn't figure out how to do it, and that was what made my decision for me: I fucking went for it.

I reached for him, my hands going to either side of his neck to bring his mouth to mine, and his lips instantly parted. I didn't hold back as Reid's arms wrapped tightly around me, keeping us crushed together, his short nails scouring my back like he couldn't get close enough. My tongue dipped inside his mouth, and I savored my first taste of him like I'd never had a chance before.

It was like coming home. The way his body fit so perfectly against mine, the way we moved in sync to take greedy sucks and licks of each other...and I knew it would be the same way once he was back in my bed.

"Ollie," he said, gripping my hair tight before diving in to tangle our tongues once more. His cock punched against mine, rock hard and begging for attention, but even though I was dying to get on my knees to suck him senseless, my self-restraint won out. I'd waited too long, had wanted him too much, and I wasn't gonna fuck this up. He was too important to me to rush things, and I wanted him to be sure of me, not just caught up in the moment.

But one thing was for damn certain—Reid Valentine was mine.

CHAPTER FOURTEEN

REID

I COULDN'T SLEEP. I tossed and turned, kicking the covers off, throwing them back on. It was that antsy feeling of wanting something you couldn't have as your mind raced to figure out a way to make it happen.

With every day I spent with Ollie, it was just another day of trying not to reach for him. I was guessing he felt the same, since he'd kept our outings public, never taking me back to his place or coming to mine. Our time at the waterfall the weekend before still weighed heavily on my mind, my lips still tingling from the kiss I hadn't been able to stop thinking about.

But he hadn't kissed me again. Not during dinner on Monday, or at the movie theater Tuesday. He'd kept his hands to himself while we jogged beside each other Wednesday, and not seeing him on Thursday when he had to work overtime had been torture. And tonight?

I let out a frustrated sigh and rolled over. The clock on my nightstand said it was one thirty. He'd dropped me off only a couple of hours earlier after round two of bowling, in which I'd fared only slightly better than the last time, but already I missed him. That emotion was something I was coming to terms with—I *missed* Ollie when he wasn't around. I missed the way he laughed. The shy way he ducked his head when I gave him a compliment. The way he was so damn nice to everyone we came across, from waiters to random people we passed on the street to my parents, who'd come out to say hello on our jog.

Even when he didn't say a word, his presence was a constant comfort, and I wished there was a way to tell him, to show him that I wanted him around. I *needed* him around, and that truth should've knocked me over like a ton of bricks, but instead, that revelation was...freeing. Falling for him again had been so effortless that I hadn't even realized it was happening, and somehow I knew that even if I'd never remembered moments from our time together before, I would've still come to this conclusion right here, right now.

As I'd gotten to know him again, things had...changed. It didn't matter that I'd never been with a guy before him. That no longer intimidated me or gave me pause. It wasn't about his gender at all, even though I'd been surprised at first at how powerfully my body reacted to the very male parts of his, parts I now craved to feel and touch. To me, he was just Ollie, my Ollie, the person who lit up the world around him with vibrant color, and yet he had no idea the effect he had on others...on me. No clue how special he was. Hell, the only fault I found with him was the fact that he was giving me too much space, when all I wanted to do was get close to him. And if I'd learned anything over the past few months, it was that you never knew when your time was up or when your life would change. It felt like it had taken forever to get to this moment, but somehow, I'd fallen for Ollie again, and I didn't want to waste another day without letting him know exactly what he had come to mean to me.

I reached for my phone and pulled up a new text message. He was probably sleeping, but if he wasn't...

Reid: Are you awake?

Almost immediately, he wrote back: **You caught me. How are you still up?**

Reid: Can't sleep.

Ollie: Everything okay?

Reid: Was thinking about you.

Ollie: Ohh. Good thoughts?

Reid: VERY good thoughts...

Ollie: Care to share?

Oh, I want to share, all right, I thought, as an idea took hold. I opened my Uber app to see there was a car less than five minutes away, so I hit *confirm pickup* and threw on some shorts and a shirt. Then I quickly brushed my teeth and headed downstairs.

Ollie: Did you fall back asleep? Damn tease.

Reid: Sorry. Got lost in those thoughts again.

Ollie: That's awfully selfish to keep it to yourself, Bluebird.

My skin tingled as I read over the nickname, and when the driver pulled up, I climbed inside the back seat, not up for conversation.

Reid: Who said I'd be keeping it to myself?

Ollie: ...I'm waiting.

Reid: I was thinking about whether or not you sleep naked.

Three dots appeared, then disappeared, then popped up again, like he kept erasing what he wrote.

Ollie: I'll tell you, but I'm curious what your conclusion was.

Reid: I remember very clearly that you never wore anything...at least when I was over.

Ollie: You're right. What else do you remember?

Reid: The sounds you make when you come. You always said my name, and it was hot as hell.
Ollie: FUCK.
Reid: I remember that too. ;)
Ollie: Christ, Reid. I think you're trying to kill me.

The driver pulled up in front of Ollie's house, and as I got out of the car, my dick pulsed in time with my heartbeat.

Reid: Not yet. Will you do me a favor?
Ollie: I'm already touching myself.

Oh *fuck*.

Reid: Open your door.
Ollie: Open my door? Why?

Less than thirty seconds later, Ollie did just that, and the astonishment on his face when he saw me standing on his porch was priceless.

"I thought we could talk about this in person instead," I said, a smile turning up one side of my mouth.

As he stood there frozen, my eyes swept over him. His wavy hair was slightly mussed on top, maybe from tossing and turning on his pillow, the same as I had, and he was bare-chested, though a fine sheen of sweat covered his pecs, like I'd just caught him in the middle of a workout. *My kind of workout*, I thought, looking down to see a pair of thin boxers peeking out from the unbuttoned jeans that sat low on his hips. It didn't do a thing to cover his arousal, and it had my desire amping up.

"Are you gonna stand there staring, or are you gonna let me in?" I said.

Still in shock, it took him a second to move aside so that I could come in.

"Good surprise?" I asked, as he shut the door.

"You have no idea."

"Oh, I think I have some idea," I said, glancing down at the way his erection hadn't subsided. *Yes, coming over was a very good decision...*

"And that's exactly why I haven't invited you over here before."

Oh...oh shit. So...bad idea?

"Would you rather I leave?" I asked.

He shook his head. "No. I don't want you to leave. Trust me, that's the last thing I want."

"But...?"

"But Reid... I'm not sure I trust myself around you if we're alone."

There. That was exactly the reaction I'd been hoping for. The look of longing was clear as day on Ollie's face as he held himself back, like he thought it was the right thing to do, when it was not at all what I wanted. Not anymore.

Even though the plan had been to launch myself at him, I needed to set his mind at ease. I wanted him to know exactly where I stood, and that me coming over wasn't some hair-trigger decision I'd regret in the morning.

Giving him some space, I turned and walked down the hall, and when I saw the piano sitting lonely in the corner, I headed straight for it.

"You bought this for me," I said, remembering what my mom had told me.

"Yes."

"For me," I murmured, spreading my hands out over the top. "Because you wanted to make me happy. Because you believe in me." I looked up. "Because you...care...about me?"

He stared at me and then nodded, and when he did, a slow melody filled my mind. I walked over and lifted the fallboard. Standing there, I played the notes as I heard them.

"That's my favorite," Ollie said quietly.

"You know this one?"

He nodded and came toward me. "You've played it for me before."

"I have?" I played a little more, and the song that came out was a tender love song, sweeter than any I could recall. "This reminds me of you."

"You said that too."

I looked up. "I wrote it for you?"

He only smiled, but that smile unlatched something inside me. Something that was ready to belong to someone else. My heart.

"Ollie, I...I've never felt this way before. Not about anyone, and certainly not about a man," I said. "That's part of the reason why I held back from you even though I knew the way you made me feel. I couldn't understand why I looked at you differently, but it all makes sense now. The memories I've been having lately, of our time together before my surgery...I felt so... I don't know. Almost carefree. Which is strange, because I should've been anything but." I looked down at where my fingers still moved across the keys, almost of their own accord. "Can I ask you something?"

"Anything."

"Did it seem like I was happy to you after my accident? Not remembering? Having a fresh slate. No baggage to weigh you down or keep you up all night?"

He took his time answering. "It certainly seemed that way. You still struggled, so it wasn't easy. You had worries for different reasons. I will say that it always surprised me how easygoing you were, and how open you seemed, not only to me, but navigating your new normal. But were you happier? I can't answer that for you, but from the outside looking in, you came off that way."

"I've thought about that a lot over the last couple of weeks. Because the thing about remembering is that you also remember everything that's been ingrained in you for years. Everything others say is right or wrong, habits you've picked up, whether good or bad. Memories can make you realize how unhappy you were. And before my accident? I was miserable."

Ollie's eyes were full of sympathy as he leaned against the side of the piano.

"That's what waking up after surgery was like," I said. "Like I'd had the most incredible dream only to find out it wasn't real. It wasn't until you came around that my world came back to life."

He sucked in a breath, and I stopped playing and folded my arms on top of the piano.

"Do you want to know what I'm more upset about than anything?" I said.

"Tell me."

"It's that I don't remember our first time," I said, staring at his lips as he bit down on them, and then I slowly perused his body. That corded neck, his strong shoulders, the tattoos that wound around his forearm. "I remember other times with you, but not our first. I don't remember how it started or where it happened. If I was the one who made the first move, or if it was you."

"That just means you get a new first," he said, his voice dropping an octave as he pushed off the piano and came to stand in front of me. His eyes had dilated like the idea of giving me another first excited him, but he wasn't going to push me. But screw that—I wanted him to push me.

"Ollie," I whispered, placing my hand on his chest. The muscle there was so firm, and it made me want to trail my fingers down to the other parts of him to remember how hard he was everywhere.

"I think...I want you to touch me," I said, my eyes dropping again to his lips. Beneath my hand, Ollie trembled.

"If you want me to touch you, you'd better be sure."

"I'm sure," I said without hesitation, and looked up at him. "Touch me, Ollie."

His hand covered mine as he searched my gaze, and then he brought my fingers up to his lips and kissed them softly—but that was the last gentle move he made. Because then, with an urgency that felt like he'd been holding back for years, he drew me toward him, his grip unyielding as one hand went around my waist and the other held the back of my head. His kiss made me dizzy, sucking the air out of my lungs, but it didn't matter that he took my breath, my tongue, even my heart, because Ollie's mouth was on mine, and nothing had ever felt so right in the world.

My nails dug into his back, and he angled his head to tangle our tongues even deeper, the velvet softness of him so intoxicating that I thought my legs would give out. When the backs of my knees stumbled into the bench, Ollie angled me slightly, and my ass hit the keys, pounding out a cacophony of notes as we devoured each other. His cock felt like steel against my lower stomach, and I lifted my right leg onto the bench to give him better access. He rubbed himself against me as my hand snaked down beneath his boxers to grab his ass.

"Fuck. Reid..."

With fumbling fingers, I shoved his jeans down his hips, and he kicked them away, his wallet and keys sliding across the kitchen floor, instantly forgotten.

"I want more," I said, breathless, and Ollie smirked against my lips.

"Then wrap your legs around me." The husky tone of his voice demanded that I comply, so when he lifted me, I circled my legs around his hips, and fuck—it was the perfect position as his dick pressed into mine. His arms went under my ass, and as he walked us back to the bedroom, I undulated against him, rubbing our cocks together in a delicious bit of friction that had my eyes practically rolling back in my head.

He threw me on the bed and I landed on my back. I lay there, trying to catch my breath as he took lube and condoms out of a side drawer and tossed them on the bed.

Oh God, I wanted this. I hadn't realized how desperately my body had been craving his until this very moment, and like he could see the desire written all over my face, Ollie stripped out of his boxers. Pushing up to my elbows, I took in the trimmed auburn curls that surrounded his long, thick shaft, and when I licked my lips, he gripped the base of his dick.

Sitting up, I peeled off my shirt and then had my shorts off in record time. I hadn't worn boxer briefs under them, which had Ollie's eyes widening. But he didn't make a move like I expected. Instead, he stared at me as he worked his erection and said, "You're the most gorgeous thing I've ever seen."

The truth in his eyes made me swallow hard before I could speak again. "Then why are you so far away?"

Ollie dropped his hand and placed a knee on the bed. His gaze ran over me from my feet to the top of my head, and when he'd climbed onto the mattress beside me, he leaned down and kissed me in a way that made me glad I was lying down.

"I've missed you," he said against my lips, as his hand stroked its way down my side. My fingers came up to caress his face, the stubble there reminding me of how good it would feel against my thighs, like he'd promised in my memory.

"I won't leave you again. I promise."

"You're mine?" he said, a small smile on his lips.

"All yours. For as long as you want me."

"Good." He nibbled and sucked on my lower lip. "Forever, then."

In all the memories I had of us together, never had I expected the enormity of how I'd feel when we finally came together. It was all so much more than what I'd merely seen, the emotions running through me putting what I thought had been a strong case of lust to shame.

His fingers wrapping around my cock brought me out of my head, my hips bucking up to chase his hand as it reached the tip before sliding back down again.

"That feels...amazing," I said on an exhale. Every time his grip moved down my dick, I had to hold my breath, because the urge to come already was too strong, and there was no way I wasn't getting inside him first before that happened. Or maybe...

"Ollie?" I stopped his wrist. "Can we try something...different?"

He sat back on his heels, a grin on his lips. "Anything you want."

I lifted myself up, and when I took his hard length in my hand, his body quivered. "I want to feel you inside me this time. It can be just this once, but it's all I can think about. You taking me."

His nostrils flared, and I could feel the blazing heat that emanated off him. "Are you sure that's what you want?" he asked, his voice so deep and thick it sounded like a growl.

"Yes," I said, swirling my thumb over the head of his cock. "That's what I want."

"Then put the condom on me."

I picked up the packet and tore it with my teeth. Then I pinched the tip and rolled it over him, wondering how it would feel to have every inch of him inside me. He didn't have to ask for the lube; I had the lid flipped open and the cool liquid pouring out into my hand in a matter of seconds, and he chuckled at my eagerness.

"I need to stretch you first," he said, swiping some of the lube from my hand with two fingers and then leaning against the headboard. "Straddle me, handsome."

I did as he said, hovering over his lap as he spread my cheeks apart with one hand, while the other came around to tease in between. Without meaning to, I tensed when one finger grazed my tight pucker, but then I forced my hips to relax and sank back down.

"That's it," he said, running his fingertip along the outside again. "Try to keep yourself relaxed for me."

With my hands on his broad shoulders, I kissed him as he continued to massage my hole, and then his lips pulled away from mine and he said, "Now breathe out."

As I exhaled, he slid a finger inside, and I had to force myself not to tense up again. The feeling was so foreign that my body wanted to reject it at first, but my mind had other ideas. I wanted this man, and I wanted him to mark me and claim me for his own. Ollie repeated the move several times, and when he added a second finger, I cursed.

"Mmm, so fucking hot, Bluebird," he said, the use of my nickname causing me to shudder as he sucked on the tender skin below my ear. All the while, he stretched me, getting me ready for the steel rod kicking against mine.

My head fell back as I got used to the intrusion, and I rolled my hips in time with his talented fingers. Then he bumped up against my prostate, and I dug my fingernails into his shoulders. "Oh fuck, Ollie. *God.* I need more. I... How do you want me?"

"Every fucking way I can have you," he said, nipping at my lobe. "But we'll start with this." He lined himself up with my hole, and then I felt the blunt head of him nudge my opening. I wasn't sure how I was going to manage to fit all of him inside, but I didn't care if I died trying.

"Let me in, Reid," he said, breathing heavy as he entered me, and then his strong hands took hold of my hips. Then he kissed me and grinned as he gave up control. "I'm all yours."

Fuck, fuck, fuck, fuck, fuck, I thought, as I breathed out and sank slowly, ever so slowly, over the top of him. He was so big, but

I'd expected the pain, welcomed it even, and it wasn't long before he was fully inside me. I went to move, but Ollie held me still as his eyes slammed shut.

"Hold on," he said, like he was the one in pain. "You feel too good. Way too damn good."

Like a cat who caught the canary, I grinned, thrilled with the fact that I could make him lose his mind. When his hold on my hips loosened, I lifted up slowly before sinking back down, relishing the way he filled me completely. It took me a few unhurried minutes of getting used to the way he felt inside me before I could move any faster, but when I did, it was *on*.

The guttural sounds escaping Ollie's throat had to be the sexiest, most gratifying thing I'd ever heard, and so was the way he'd pretended to give me control by straddling him, when really, he was the one fully in charge.

And Ollie fully in charge was so fucking hot.

With his hands busy setting the pace, I reached down to stroke myself in time with his thrusts, but *shit*, it was too much to have him inside me while I worked my cock. The orgasm came out of nowhere, spilling onto Ollie's stomach in hot white jets of cum that seemed never-ending.

"Oh fuck, Reid," he said, groaning as his hips moved faster, the rhythm becoming erratic as he got closer to his climax. I was grateful in that moment that he'd wanted us face to face for this, because it was then that Ollie came with a roar, my name on his tongue and his head falling back, and that was a view I wouldn't have wanted to miss for the world. He was simply spectacular in his ecstasy, his skin flushed and his green eyes almost completely eclipsed by his blown pupils.

Before he could catch his breath again, I gripped the back of his neck and stole a kiss. Still inside me, he wrapped me up in his huge arms, holding me so tight that I didn't think he'd ever let go. I hoped he wouldn't.

"That was perfect," I said, leaning back just enough so I could look into his eyes. "You're perfect."

He was the missing piece, the part of me I had felt was lost, to the point where I'd lashed out at everyone and everything out of sheer frustration. I never would've imagined that Ollie would be the one to give me the answers I'd sought. That he was the only one who could make me feel whole again. It was that truth that had set me free. I'd never felt more complete or more loved than I did in Ollie's arms. And now that I knew my place, I never planned to leave.

CHAPTER FIFTEEN

REID

I WASN'T SURE if what I was hearing was a memory playing out in my dream, or if it was actually happening, but as the fog of sleep cleared and I woke up, the house was silent.

Ollie lay sleeping on his side facing me, and I smiled as I watched him breathe, his expression so peaceful. One of his arms was curled beneath his pillow, and the other lay on the bed between us, almost like he'd been reaching out for me.

It had been a full day of reconnecting since I'd shown up on his doorstep in the early hours of the morning, and even though my body ached to feel him against me once more, we could both use a few hours of rest. Or he could. I was too busy thinking of the song I'd played earlier, the same one from my dream just now, and I quietly slid out of the bed, threw on my shorts, and closed the door behind me so I wouldn't wake him up. I'd told him the song reminded me of the way he made me feel. Like coming home. Never was that truer than the way I'd felt in the last twenty-four hours wrapped up in him.

When I got to the kitchen, the sight that greeted me made me chuckle. Ollie's jeans were still in a heap on the floor by the piano, which sent a thrill of excitement through me as I recalled them coming off in the heat of the moment. I folded them and placed them on top of the counter, only to see his wallet and keys still strewn across the tile. Nothing else seemed to have fallen out, so I picked them both up, and when I did, a folded-up slip of paper fell out of his wallet. It was so wrinkled and thin, like it'd been opened too many times, that it unfolded as it hit the floor. I frowned as I reached for it, taken aback to see my own handwriting on the torn-off page.

It was a letter to Ollie. And as I read it, all of the worry and fear from that day came rushing back with startling clarity, and I collapsed to my knees.

"Can I have a pen and some paper? Hurry, please," I said to the nurse before she left the room.

My parents stood beside the bed looking down at me with concern and fear in their eyes, though they were trying to hide it with their soothing words.

"You're here and the doctors will get this all sorted," Mom said, holding my hand and rubbing the top of it. "It's going to be fine."

"I know," I said, even though I didn't know, and I didn't think it would be fine. Dread filled every inch of me, a sense of foreboding I couldn't shake.

"It's a good thing you were with Ollie when it happened," my father said.

Ollie... I needed to talk to Ollie. I hadn't wanted him to leave the room when my parents arrived, but he'd graciously given them the time to be with me while he was... Where was he? I wanted him to come back. Everything was happening so fast, and all I wanted was a few quiet minutes with him.

The nurse came back in and handed me a pen and notepad,

and as I held them, I tried to calm my mind enough to write what I needed to in case I didn't get a chance to see him before I went into surgery. In case...anything should happen.

Nothing will happen, *I told myself.* Everything is going to work out.

That would've been easier to believe if another crushing headache didn't have me wincing and my mom calling out for the nurse again.

"I'm fine." *I tried to wave them off, because, fuck, I was terrified, and I didn't want them to see it. With the way my heart felt like it was stuttering with every beat, I was surprised the monitors I'd been hooked up to hadn't already alerted them to my fear. I hadn't wanted Ollie to see it either, but there was never any way for me to hide from him.*

"What are you doing, baby?" *my mom asked.*

"Just give me one sec."

Thankfully, she didn't ask any other questions, and settled into one of the chairs beside me, giving me the space I needed to pour my heart out onto the page.

Ollie,

I know you're worried. And maybe I am too.

Strike that. I'm a lot worried. There. I admitted it. I'm fucking terrified, but I was trying not to show you.

It doesn't seem fair that I'm back here, but we haven't gone through these last few weeks to give up now.

I just found you. I'm not losing you, and I won't forget you, no matter what happens.

But if, somehow, the worst-case scenario comes true, I need you to promise me you won't give up on me.

Help me remember.

Help me find my way back to you.

Love,
Your Bluebird

I tore off the paper and folded it four times, and then I closed my eyes so no one would see me cry. I didn't understand why, but it felt like a part of me was dying, and I didn't know how to stop it from happening. I just hoped that somehow, some way, Ollie wouldn't let me go...

"You came back to me."

I looked up through a haze of tears as Ollie pushed off the doorway and crossed over to where I was sitting on the tile. He knelt beside me and wiped my tears away with both hands. I stared at him, blinking fast, trying to clear my vision as I sat there holding the heavily creased paper with shaking hands. "You kept this..."

"It goes everywhere I do. I told you I'd keep you with me."

I took a deep, quivering breath. "This whole time...I felt like... I missed you somehow. It didn't make any sense to me, because I didn't know you, or I didn't think I did. But..." I looked down at the letter again, the one that only confirmed how strongly I'd felt about him then, and how right it all was now. "I felt like I should."

Tears fell down Ollie's face to match mine, but when he didn't wipe them away, I set the letter aside and took his face in my hands. I kissed away every salty drop, and when I was done, I rested my forehead against his.

"I promised I'd wake up to you. It may not have been right away, but I'm awake now, Ollie. I'm awake, and I see you. I see us."

He lifted his head then and kissed me, a long, deep, searing kiss that scorched my insides, leaving nothing in its wake.

"I love you," I said. "I should've told you that before my surgery, because there's nothing truer in this world than the fact that I love you, Oliver McFadden. Every perfect inch of you. You never stopped believing in me, even when I lost hope in myself, even when I pushed you away...even when I hurt you. But you... you love so fiercely. You see the good in the world because you *are* the good in the world."

Ollie brushed the wetness from the corner of my eye with his thumb, and I could only stare at him in wonder before shaking my head.

"I don't understand how you can look at me like that," I said.

"Like what?"

"With your entire heart in your eyes."

"Because I love you," he said. "You own me, Bluebird. Completely. You always have, and you always will." His lips skimmed against my knuckles in a light caress. "I loved you the first time I saw you in your cardinal pin, before you even knew I existed. Way before I even knew your name. There's nothing I wouldn't do for you. No lengths I wouldn't go to keep you safe. To keep you happy. That's all I'll ever want in this life—to make you happy. To love you with all that I am." He choked up at the end, and I couldn't help wrapping my arms around his neck and letting him feel my response, and the way my heart soared at his words, with a kiss.

It was beautiful. It was perfect. It was worth every ounce of heartbreak and every scared and confused thought I'd ever had. To be with Ollie, I would go through it all again, over and over, just for the moments like this, where I felt like my heart was going to burst from the overflow of love he gave to me.

"Reid?"

"Hmm?"

"Can I ask how you ended up on the kitchen floor?"

I laughed and pointed to his pants, keys, and wallet on the counter. "You went wild getting naked for me, that's how. Stuff all over the floor," I teased.

"You're not complaining, are you?"

"Hell no. Actually, that reminds me—there's something else about you that I forgot to mention I love."

"My bowling skills?"

"It does involve balls, yes."

"Huh. You haven't seen me play tackle football yet."

"No, but now I have something else to look forward to. But Ollie? I just have to tell you... I really, really love"—I moved in like I was going to kiss him—"your cock." He busted out laughing as my lips twitched in amusement. "I know. Words I never thought I'd say, but it's true. I've never seen a more impressive dick."

"Uh, I would think fucking not," he said. "But I, for one, am very happy to hear how much you love my cock. As a matter of fact, I think you should spend some time letting my cock know just how much you love it."

"I dunno... I see lots of long, hard hours spent getting better reacquainted. You sure you're up for that?"

He lifted his eyebrows and looked down at his lap to where his pants had tented. "Really? Do you have to ask?"

"Not anymore I don't," I said, and gave him another kiss. "You belong to me now. I'm taking you any time I want to."

"I think I like this side of you."

"I hope so. Because I plan to be around for the long haul. There's no getting rid of me now."

"I guess I can get rid of the chains in the basement, then."

"Hmm." I sucked his lower lip into my mouth. "Maybe don't get rid of those just yet."

"Is now the time you tell me you're secretly a kinky bastard?"

"I don't think I should tell you. Maybe I'll show you."

Ollie groaned and pulled me onto his lap. "How did we get on this subject? I thought you were going to tell me you came in here to play our song."

"Our song, huh?"

His eyes twinkled. "Isn't it?"

My heart melted a little as I realized I'd fallen in love with the most incredible person I'd ever met—a person that just so happened to be a man. And what was more? I fucking loved it. I loved the way my body caught fire every time he was near, and I loved the way he loved me with every fiber of his being. That's just who Ollie was: someone who loved completely. And somehow, against all odds, it was *me* he'd chosen to give himself to. And I planned to choose him back, again and again, every day for the rest of our lives.

"I'm not sure how I got so lucky. I wouldn't have even known how to wish for you," I said.

Ollie tightened his hold on me and held my face in his hands. "I don't need a wish." He brushed a kiss against my lips before saying the words I would cherish forever: "I got everything I ever wanted...when you came back to me."

EPILOGUE

REID - TWO YEARS LATER

"**O**H WOW, THIS place is *packed*," Anna said, peeking out of the heavy red velvet curtain at the Maxwell Center for the Arts, to where over twenty-five hundred seats were being filled for my sold-out inaugural concert.

"An-na." Ollie gave her the *look*, and she quickly shut the curtain.

"Oops," she said. "I mean, uh, wow, no one wanted to see you play tonight, huh?"

Oh Jesus. Where's a vomit bucket when you need one?

Ollie just shook his head as he put his arm around her neck like he was going to give her a noogie. "Why don't you go make sure no one's taken our seats, would ya? Troublemaker."

"No, my hair," she shrieked, wiggling out of his hold, and then she launched herself at me. "You're going to be amazing, Reid. Don't even think about all those people out there."

"Thanks, Banana. I'll picture them all in their underwear."

Ollie sent the *look* my way, and I backtracked. "Okay, maybe not in their underwear."

As Anna went back out into the audience, I took in a couple of deep breaths and stretched out my fingers.

"Come here—let me fix your tie," Ollie said, and I stood still in front of him as he straightened the black bow at my neck, followed by the cardinal wings on my lapel. "Don't be nervous. You've got this."

"I'm not nervous." When he raised an eyebrow, I exhaled. "Why would I be nervous? There are only a couple thousand people and a handful of producers out there who could make or break me. No biggie. Really."

"Exactly. But just because you've been working for this for a year and a half doesn't mean your whole career depends on tonight."

"Gee, thanks, babe. You're as bad as Anna."

"Hey, you've gone through worse and come out the other side."

"Are you referring to when I married you?" I teased. Ollie's mouth fell open, a retort on his tongue, when I laughed and then planted a kiss on his lips. "I'm kidding. You meant the head through the glass thing, right?"

He shook his head and gripped my waist, pulling me flush against him so I could feel the way his cock pulsed through his dress pants. "I'll remember that later."

"I was hoping you'd say that." I tugged on his lobe with my teeth, and he shivered in my arms. It never got old, the effect I had on my man, and neither did the intoxicating scent of him, nothing but pheromones that made me want to lick his neck. "You keep distracting me, and I'm gonna have to cancel the concert."

That made him pull away, holding me at arm's length. "Not in a million years. I can wait two hours."

I looked down at the way the front of his pants tented. "I don't know about that."

"Trust me, watching you play is the sweetest kind of torture. Foreplay, if you will."

"Really?"

"Mmm. Something about knowing where those talented fingers of yours will end up later..."

It was my jaw's turn to drop, and he laughed at my expression.

"Just know that's what I'll be thinking about tonight."

"You bastard. I have to go out there in five minutes."

"Then I guess you'd better practice your self-restraint now."

"I had no idea you were so evil. Are you sure *you* haven't bumped your head lately?"

"This is payback for the other night." When I furrowed my brow, he said, "You. Showing up at the station. Not a stitch of clothing on underneath that fucking trench coat."

"Ohh, yes, it's all coming back to me now. Emphasis on coming." I hummed as I remembered the look on Ollie's face when I took him to the back and opened the coat. "That was a good night."

"*Two minutes*," the stage manager said as she passed by, and instantly the nerves were back, the panic settling in something fierce.

"Oh God. What if they hate it?"

"Impossible."

I gave him a solemn look. "Be serious."

"I am being serious. A contemporary infusion of classics and rock songs? What's not to love? They're going to be begging for more, just wait."

"It's been so long since I've performed. I think I've forgotten how."

"What did you tell me once? That when you step on stage and start to play, everyone fades into the background. Right?"

My lips tipped up on one side. "*Almost* everyone."

"That's right. I'll be the one cheering you on from the front row so loud it'll be obnoxious, I promise." I chuckled as he lifted my hand to his lips and kissed my wedding band. "You always make your husband proud. Always." Then he took my chin and gave me a soft kiss that lingered—one I was looking forward to continuing tonight.

"I love you," I whispered as I closed my eyes and rested my forehead against his. His hands squeezed mine, firm and steady. Always my rock.

"I love you, Reid. This is the beginning of your dreams coming true. I feel it."

"No. You're wrong about that," I said, lifting my head to meet his eyes. "My dream began before I met you. In that little coffee aisle at Joe's, when you saw me and what we could be before I even knew to look up."

Ollie's eyes glassed over, and I kissed his full lips again.

"Thank you for saving me," I said, and I meant that in every way. He'd not only saved my life, but he'd saved my soul. He'd saved my hope when I had none. The man I was lucky enough to wake up next to every day had brought me back to life, and as I took a deep breath and stepped out onto the stage, I knew that with him by my side, lifting me up as I did him, I'd never fall.

And *that* was what dreams were made of.

THANK YOU

Thank you all so much for reading **Forget Me Not** and **Remember Me When**. It was an honor to bring Ollie and Reid to life and to share them with you.

Who would've thought that sitting at a red light watching an ambulance pass by a gas station would've been the catalyst for these guys? It's true what we always say—inspiration comes from EVERYwhere. Sometimes stories must be told, or they'll sabotage every other idea you have until you throw your hands up and agree. This was one of those times, and I couldn't be more proud of how it all turned out in the end.

Thank you for sharing this journey with me.

Lots of love,

Brooke

If you enjoyed **The Unforgettable Duet**, please consider leaving a review on the site you purchased the book from. Ollie & Reid would be ever so grateful. <3

If you'd like more stories from Brooke, make sure to check them out at www.BrookeBlaine.com.

ALSO BY BROOKE BLAINE

The Unforgettable Duet
Forget Me Not
Remember Me When

South Haven Series
A Little Bit Like Love

L.A. Liaisons Series
Licked
Hooker
P.I.T.A.

Romantic Suspense
Flash Point

PresLocke Series
Co-Authored with Ella Frank
Aced
Locked
Wedlocked

Standalones

Co-Authored with Ella Frank

Sex Addict

Shiver

Wrapped Up in You

ABOUT THE AUTHOR

Brooke Blaine is a *USA Today* Bestselling Author of contemporary romance that ranges from comedy to suspense to erotic. The latter has scarred her conservative Southern family for life, bless their hearts.

If you'd like to get in touch with her, she's easy to find - just keep an ear out for the Rick Astley ringtone that's dominated her cell phone for years. Or you can reach her at www.BrookeBlaine.com.

Where to find Brooke:
Join Brooke's Newsletter at www.BrookeBlaine.com for the latest news!
Brooke & Ella's Naughty Umbrella on Facebook for fans of Brooke Blaine & Ella Frank
The M/M Daily Grind on Facebook for M/M fans
Book + Main Bites
bookandmainbites.com/brookeblaine

www.BrookeBlaine.com
brooke@brookeblaine.com

Facebook: facebook.com/BrookeBlaine.Writer

Instagram: instagram.com/brookeblaine1
Twitter: twitter.com/BrookeBlaine1

ACKNOWLEDGMENTS

As always, the person keeping me from completely losing my marbles (though I'm still missing quite a few), is Ella Frank. I swear my books would probably never see the light of day if she wasn't the one reassuring me that "they're good enough, smart enough, and doggone-it, people will like (love!) it." Ella, I know I drive you nuts with the my procrastination (I drive myself crazy too), and you are a saint for putting up with me. And writing with me! Well, a saint or a sucker, your choice. ;) I love you, woman, and I can't wait to work with you on our next project. Just think—Sydney & Taylor soon! #Rewards (Ps - GET OUT OF THE CAR, ANNA! YOU COCKBLOCKER.)

Shannon with Shanoffi Designs did such an incredible job bringing Ollie & Reid to life on these covers & teasers, and I have to say thank you, Shannon! You nailed it from the beginning, and I so appreciate you always doing such gorgeous work.

Speaking of beautiful covers, Forget Me Not features model Kevin Hessam (His flrst cover! Yay!), with photography by the always amazing Eric Battershell (Eric Battershell Photography). We've collaborated on several covers now, and the images never fail to be utter perfection. Cheers to many more!

Thank you also to Darren Birks Photography (CoversUnleashed.com) for the photo of model Zak Leete for Remember Me When.

    Both of these covers helped me visualize my guys as I wrote their story, and I can't stress enough how important a cover is, not only for readers as they choose their next read, but also for an author. I mean, come on, gorgeous men to stimulate productivity? #Win

My editor, Arran McNicol, who proved his worth a million times over with this book in particular. Ps - Wakanda forever.

Jenn, Sarah, & Brooke of Social Butterffy PR - You ladies always have my back, and for that I'm grateful. You do so much behind the scenes, and I appreciate you taking hate mail for the team. Bahaha I kiiiid! I love you guys, but the next time any of you go to London or Paris without me, there will be words. STRONG WORDS! Muah!

I need to say a special thank you to three women who took the time to answer so many of my questions regarding their work as paramedics and how they would treat medical emergencies. Many times, we writers take creative liberties with our stories to make them flt what we have in our head, but it's also important to nail those little details that really make a story feel realistic. So, Jamie Farruggia Plume, Julie Boswell, and Connie Griffln: a big thank you and tackle hugs! If you read the book, I hope you enjoy your Easter eggs. ;)

And to my kickass review team of faaabulous hookers, my naughty brellas, & the m/m daily grinders—I'm so thankful for your support, kind words, hilarious stories and posts, and your friendship.

Bloggers! Readers! You all never cease to amaze me. Each time you pick up my book, each time you share it with your friends or on Instagram or Facebook, every time you review on Goodreads or Amazon, and especially when you make those gorgeous little graphics that I can't help but share immediately—you blow my mind every time and with every gesture, every kind word, and I can't thank you enough. Many of you have been with me since the first time I hit publish, and the fact that you've stayed through allll these different genres and stories means I should probably send you crazy pills. Or hugs. Crazy pills and hugs? And chocolate?

Thank you all so much for reading Forget Me Not and Remember Me When. It was an honor to bring Ollie and Reid to life and to share them with you. Who would've thought that sitting at a red light watching an ambulance pass by a gas station would've been the catalyst for these guys? It's true what we always say—inspiration comes from EVERYwhere. Sometimes stories must be told, or they'll sabotage every other idea you have until you throw your hands up and agree. This was one of those times, and I couldn't be more proud of how it all turned out in the end. Thank you for sharing this journey with me.

Lots of love,

Brooke

Made in the USA
San Bernardino, CA
05 August 2019